# DOUBLE TAKE

Taking photographs at a wedding shouldn't have been dangerous. But when a bank raid takes place close to the church, more people are interested in the wedding photos than just the bridal party.

Len Podmore, the photographer, isn't the sort of person to sit back and forget it when his negatives and proofs are stolen. He wants them back, but he's up against two rival gangs of crooks, and when you're squeezed in the middle, the situation isn't too comfortable. Especially when Len's not certain which side the police are on.

With a mixture of aggression and sardonic humour, Len steers a hectic course between bluff and counter-bluff, and if the bodies continue to appear it isn't his fault. Is it?

# DOUBLE TAKE

## Roger Ormerod

·BLACK·
DAGGER
·CRIME·

First published 1980
by
Robert Hale Ltd

This edition 2006 by BBC Audiobooks Ltd
published by arrangement with
the author's estate

ISBN 10: 1 4056 8543 3
ISBN 13: 978 1 405 68543 6

**British Library Cataloguing in Publication Data available**

Printed and bound in Great Britain by
Antony Rowe Ltd., Chippenham, Wiltshire

# *One*

I hate weddings. You don't get another chance, and there's nothing, absolutely nothing, you can control, especially the bride, and it's on her you are concentrating. The groom too, of course, but it's the bride's day. I hate, particularly, weddings in June, though this has grown on me since that one day in that special June. It was, you see, my first wedding.

This particular church, St Godolph's, was just off the main square, with traffic continuously along three sides of the open churchyard. I can ignore traffic, but the paths were used as pedestrian short-cuts, and at eleven on a hot June morning the grassed expanse was an invitation to rollicking children and basking adults. And when it became evident that a wedding was imminent, the crowds grew.

I set up my stand with the Hasselblad for the groups, checked my exposures, and waited. I was using the Canon, hand-held, with the f/1.4 lens, waiting for the first arrivals. With all those kids around I did not dare move far from the tripod, but fortunately the Gothic doorway was only a few yards from the old iron gateway where they'd all appear. I wasn't keen on the background beyond that gateway, the Co-op the other side of the street and the bank just a little way along. The light was dreadful, harsh, the shadows hacked out in the buttresses. I was wishing I'd checked with the bride. It'd be hell if she was in white and the groom in dark blue, say. Sweat was running down the small of my back, and traffic streamed across my background. I just had to hope there wouldn't be a glaring red bus in any of the shots.

They began to arrive in large cars, two Jags, one white, doing a shuttle service. I got a shot of everybody, just in case, darting sideways from time to time to rescue my tripod from the junior vandals. I was poised for the groom and best man. A maroon Daimler slid into the kerb. Two young men got out, one short, one tall. The Daimler had parked just behind a white Police patrol car with a red stripe along it. I cursed him. There was no way I could exclude that patrol car from the background from where I was standing. I could only assume he'd stopped to watch the fun, neglecting his duties no doubt. There was no time to go and shuffle him off. Things were happening.

The shorter one must have been the groom, Martin Astel, the taller one his elder brother. The groom had compromised between a rebellious desire for patched jeans and beads and the bride's for a sombre suit, and wore a vaguely matching outfit of slacks and jacket with no lapels, but had retained his beads and the bangles. His elder brother was in the navy blue suit I'd dreaded, though on the best man it wasn't critical. But he disapproved, whether of his brother's dress or the marriage I couldn't tell. No gesture of mine affected his scowl, and he misunderstood my sign because he responded; one negative I wouldn't be able to use. But I got one of their actual entrance, with that blasted Police car in the background. There seemed to be one man behind the wheel.

6

Didn't they have mates? Perhaps he'd stopped only for his partner to visit the gents across the square, in which case he'd be moving on directly.

No such luck. The cars began piling in on each other, the Jags and the Daimler, and a Rolls sedately aged, and in they streamed, grinning fiercely, official guests of bride and groom, and by that time I'd found an awkward position almost behind a tree, from which the patrol car was not in the frame. Then at last came the bride and her father, Ruźa Ješić and poppa Ješić. She was in powder blue, which gave me a chance with the highlights, and I began to feel better about it all. At least the shots after the ceremony could be posed, and the reception was going to be flash anyway.

The vicar had requested no photographs inside the church. He was the big noise around there, so much so that he had even dictated to the bride the firm of photographers she must use, the only ones he would allow in his churchyard for that purpose. If it hadn't been for the illness of two of that firm's partners, I wouldn't have been handed the commission. I was wondering what the vicar's pay-off was going to be when I heard the organ warning me to be ready, and wound on the Hasselblad.

The gunshots came when we were on the groups. Ruźa had been a darling, smiling without strain, and she'd persuaded her new husband at least to button up his shirt, so that part was all right. But I discovered that the police driver's mate was back from the gents. Blast him, he even got into one of my groups. There he was, in my viewfinder, grinning just behind one of the bridesmaids, in his blue summer shirt with the shoulder tabs, bare-headed, so he must have left his cap on the passenger's

7

seat in the car. So maybe he was a friend of the family, determined to get in on the wedding in spite of being on duty. That would explain the car, still waiting in the street, but if he was neglecting his duties he'd have some explaining to do, because the shots came just after that picture was taken.

You've heard of gunshots being taken for backfires. But they are not alike. I knew it was gunfire, two different kinds, one a bark and one a roar, and they were followed immediately by screams. A car howled away, there were running feet, and I stumbled over my tripod, nearly taking it over. When I looked, the Police car had gone. I did not see the policeman in shirt sleeves again, not that day anyway.

Weddings are serious things, and not to be disrupted by minor outside influences. My photographs were also serious. By exercising furious concentration I managed to divert the interest from the clamouring background, and somehow we were able to complete the group shots. By that time there was chaos in the square. Police vehicles were everywhere, traffic and pedestrians were being marshalled, and ambulance sirens cut their way through the din. My happy group clustered, and gestured in distressed animation, then stood around mournfully. But of course there was the reception to attend, and nothing was to be gained by hanging around. Ruźa Ješić, now Astel, was managing a brave smile, so they all smiled, the Ješićs probably from an inherited stubbornness of spirit.

The police thoughtfully produced a clear lane for the wedding vehicles, and I ran for my Prefect in the car park round the corner. I learned from passers-by that a bank cashier had been shot in the neck and a large haul made in bank notes. Allowing for exaggeration, I decided that a minor wound might have been received and fifty quid stolen. I was wrong, it turned out.

Naive as I was at that time, I believed the reception would be easy, a time to relax. With an automatic flash and the Canon at f/11, it should have been no more than frame and fire. But I'd counted without the radios. Every time I raised the camera, there was somebody with a radio to his ear, or bent over one. They were all tuned to the local radio station, which had a reporter on the spot at the bank. They had what seemed to me to be a morbid interest in the robbery. We even had to prise the groom from the white Jag in the car park, which appeared to have radio facilities with a police channel.

"He's right on their heels," he cried, his eyes startled and his hand firm on the door frame.

We dragged him free. I said: "It's time for the cake-cutting," and was surprised to hear my own tone of severity. "There'll be plenty of time for the news later."

"No there won't."

And I blushed. You can see how harassed I was becoming.

The cake-cutting went well. At least, the cake became cut, though instead of the murmurs of encouragement and the cheers the crowd buzzed with such remarks as: "He's homing in half the county force," and, "they'll be trapped with the stuff on 'em."

Fortunately the camera did not record the words, though the groom's set teeth did not indicate the hardness of the icing, and poor Ruža's smile was fixed, her eyes glazed.

Now there was a girl. What'd she have been? Twenty-four or five, slim, maybe five-five, and dark . . . Her eyes were brown, her hair black, her skin a beautiful matt olive. Perhaps it was the way she'd done her hair, but her face seemed squat, as wide as it was deep, and when she smiled—a real one, I mean, not the agonised one I was forced to record—her cheeks glowed and her eyes danced . . . and there I was, trying to concentrate on my work!

Somehow we got through the toasts, and I was able to relax enough to sample a Riesling that hadn't come from a storeshelf. I even managed a word with Ruźa. We touched glasses in a silent toast to her eyes, and she said:

"You're not the man we saw."

"They passed the commission to me." I there and then decided to excel in this job if never again. "I'm new around here."

But she was staring worriedly beyond my shoulder for her new husband, who was no doubt in the yard with the white Jag and the police cross-talk. I couldn't see the best man, who should have been keeping his brother under control. I drifted away and began packing up my stuff, suddenly anxious to confirm that my negatives were OK, and that I hadn't done something stupid like leaving the lens cap on throughout. In the centre of the floor there was beginning a wild circle of dancing which I assumed to be a Yugoslavian fertility rite, with somebody going wild on an accordion. I'd have liked to have stayed and taken a few shots just for myself, but I was a working man, and when you work for yourself there's no let-up.

The Prefect refused to start, so I banged the petrol pump with a spanner, and after a few more turns the engine caught. I fought it back to my place in Duke Street. I have four rooms over a tobacconist's and a television hire place, with my living quarters above the two that I'd converted to studio and darkroom. That gave me two blanked-out windows over which I'd spread the words: PODMORE PHOTOGRAPHIC. Three months I'd been there, and business had been lousy. I'd advertised in the local rag, but you'd have difficulty finding my miserable doorway between the two shops, and the prospect of those straight, walled-in wooden stairs is not inviting. I was saving up for a carpet and a bit of fancy paintwork, with some of my exhibition shots framed on the walls to lure you up to the studio. When you call round, I hope it'll be ready.

It was nearly five when I got back there. There were no messages. The black tom which had adopted me had found his way into the darkroom again and nested in a developing tray. I let him stay. A black cat does no harm in the dark. His green eyes had no trace of light to reflect while I spooled the two 35-mm lengths and the two 120 lengths from the Hasselblad, dumped them in my tall tank, and got the lid on. The tall tank just about filled my requirements at that time. Then, in full light, I prepared the colour developer, stop-bath, hardener and fixer, aiming for a control temperature of 24°C. It's the first stage that really matters, the temperature control. Then you can relax a bit. The cat watched with fascination.

I had four lengths of perfect negs. At that stage you can judge only from gradation, because the colours as well as the black and whites are reversed, light yellow for dark purple, and dark green for a pink—that sort of thing. But I was happy, whistling a few bars of Schubert

11

as I hung them in the drying cupboard.

"And if I ever catch you in *there*, mate," I told the cat, "it's out, with my foot behind you."

Then we went upstairs and had our tea.

I wasn't sure how he got in, though there was a small window stuck permanently open in my tiny pantry, so that he must have arrived over the roofs, but how he got up there, three flights up, I couldn't imagine. Apart from that pantry, there was a miniature bedroom and a dining-kitchen affair with a cooker in the corner. We had poached egg on toast and Kit-E-Kat, me the egg. I read the evening paper, which had been lying in my tiny hallway downstairs, but there was very little news of the robbery. Only what I already knew. I'd missed the news on the BBC, and hunted round the dial for the local station. Then got it . . .

". . . the car was apparently driven off the road, and first reports are of three men being found at the scene of the accident. The police spokesman has not revealed whether they were captured alive, but reports are reaching us that they were dead when found. Attempts to interview the two police officers in the patrol car which chased the getaway car across two counties have been unsuccessful, and Chief Superintendent Parker has refused to comment.

"And now, news from Argentina, where . . ."

I shut him off. No news of the extent of the robbery or the injuries at the bank. Perhaps that was past history. You miss things in a darkroom.

It was nearly seven. I could have wandered round to the Black Bull, or I could . . . hell, why not? Get the proofs run off, and I'd really know if I'd caught the shade of her skin and the colour of her eyes. The cat and I went down to the darkroom.

Black cats are murder to photograph—did you know? One day I'll have a real go at him and try to get the pink insides of his ears.

You don't mess around with proofs. It's just a matter of running off two of each with the drum processor—one for them and one for my files—using an average negative as a guide and not testing each one for filter and exposure, though I must admit that with one or two I really tried. There were flecks of gold in her eyes.

I had fifty-three presentable prints out of the eighty-seven I'd taken, to offer the bride and her friends—I hoped for a few orders on the side—seventeen of which gave me cause for pride. Fifty-three, that is, if you count the one marred by that blasted grinning copper.

That night I slept deeply, and the cat didn't go home, relaxing I suppose in my personal contented pride. His nose was stuck under my chin when I woke up.

You will realise how inexperienced I was when I tell you that I took round the proofs myself. The professional and impersonal way is to slip them into the post, with an illustrated folder of the albums and mounts available, and a price list. But I had a free morning, and it never occurred to me that by that time the happy couple should be away on their honeymoon.

But they were not. At least, *she* was not. It was Ruźa who opened the door to me.

The Jeśićs had bought an old Victorian mansion, probably in the 1940s, when the whole tribe had fled from their native country. Now it was decrepit, and stucco was peeling off everywhere, paint from the front door. It was a big and heavy door, and Ruźa seemed tiny in the opening. She was also, surprisingly, shocked to see me.

"I've brought the proofs," I said, waving the envelope and grinning with shame, because it occurred to me that my behaviour could be construed as over-eagerness for my money. "I was sure you'd want to see them."

"But how could you know . . ." She bit her lip. "You'd better come in."

There was a feeling of hushed quiet in the house, and yet I had the impression that normally the walls would echo with laughter and relaxed pandemonium. It was that sort of quiet, like an empty concert hall. She led me along the echoing, peeling passages towards the rear of the house, and into a noble room with a high, carved ceiling and a huge bay window overlooking a wildly-grown garden.

They were all there, the Jeśićs in quantity and the Astels—at least, the best man, if not the groom—and one or two in-laws and stray relatives. I was conducted formally on an introduction tour, Momma and Poppa Jeśić, she a dumpy and placid matron with a strange veil over her hair, and he a gaunt giant with a huge mouth and a drooping moustache, all gestures and baggy trousers, and then the best man, now finally identified as Comus Astel. He nodded unsmilingly as we shook hands, and I realised his scowl as he'd entered that church gate might have been habitual. I wondered what worried him. The bridesmaid whom I'd particularly noticed, because her blushes at the sight of a lens had disconcerted me, turned out to be Ruźa's younger sister, Ljubica. I hope I've got the spelling correct—it sounded like Shoobeeka. She was clinging possessively to the arm of a shy young man called Danny Summers, so obviously a new acquisition that she refused to let him out of her sight.

They had been sitting in odd chairs around a table on which was scattered a pile of newspapers. Now they took their seats again, and were so plainly repressed by my presence that I almost turned and ran.

"I see they got away with a hundred and eighty thousand," I said, gesturing to the paper and trying to ease the tension.

"Not exactly got away," said Poppa Ješić severely.

Comus Astel moved across the room. He alone, apart from me, was still standing, seeming too restless to sit. He moved one hand impatiently. "We don't know that. The police haven't said they recovered the money."

Ješić waved his arms in exasperation. "Of course they've got it."

"The gentleman," put in Momma Ješić, "is a guest." She was gentle, but underlying it was a tone of authority.

At once Ješić smiled in vast politeness, and Ruža put in: "He has brought the proofs."

They stared at the envelope in her hand, helplessly. What the hell were proofs? Proofs of what?

"My wedding photographs," said Ruža in soft admonition.

I smiled ridiculously, looking round the circle. It had become embarrassing. If I'd imagined anything—and yes I had—it had been a cosy scene with Ruža on one hand, her husband Martin on the other, and me saying: "This, I think, is a pleasant shot." Or something like that. But that was shattered against the rock of their indifference, and Martin Astel was not there. And Ruža

15

had not left on her honeymoon. Good Lord, I thought, I've put my foot in it. The groom's absconded, and here I am with the wedding shots.

"I'll leave you to look through them," I faltered, feeling a complete fool, and nobody said otherwise, so I left. Ruža took me to the front door. She smiled. "I can't wait to see them," she whispered. The glow of her warmed me. How *could* he have left her?

The door closed behind me. The car wouldn't start. I dented the pump body with my spanner. It coughed to life.

I drove away, recalling that the conversation had not touched on Martin Astel at all, but on the bank robbery.

If you edge the car down a narrow alleyway off Duke Street, and manage to negotiate the space between the end wall of a garage and an old outside toilet belonging to the tobacconist, you find yourself on a square patch of ash, where I'm allowed to leave the Prefect at no extra charge. There I parked it and unbolted the petrol pump, and took it up the back stairs to my rooms at the top, then stripped it on the kitchen table. The cat wasn't keen on the smell of petrol, and disappeared.

I spent half the afternoon discovering how to take it apart, and the other half how to put it together again. I'd blown out the filters and things, and reckoned it would work, if some fathead hadn't dented the casing. Then I started to take it down the back stairs to mate it with its car.

These stairs come past the far end of the corridor in which I have my studio. I have a bell push that buzzes upstairs, and it hadn't warned me. Yet under the edge of the studio door, my eyes at that time being level with the floor, I caught a glint of light. That studio is completely dark, as you have to control what photographic light you need, so it wasn't a trick of the declining sun. I paused. A customer? But why hadn't he rung?

I approached the door. It was an inch from its latch. I put my hand to it and slid it open.

A tall man with broad shoulders was rifling the top drawer of my filing cabinet. It was the only drawer with anything in to rifle, and contained only the folders of my first seventeen jobs, and number eighteen, the Ješić wedding. He was using a torch, and I caught very little of his shape by the reflected light. But he was big. A lot bigger than me. I threw the petrol pump at his head, and missed.

At once he turned. The torch was straight in my eyes. I charged at it. I was furious. That was my property he was interfering with. I went at him without thought. Sometimes, when anger overwhelms me, I don't stop to think.

He stepped sideways. The torch caught me behind the ear and I shot forward with my own momentum straight through the door into my darkroom. The door slammed behind me and I finished up sitting against the far wall in a daze.

The cat jumped down from the bench and purred in my ear, and all I could think was that in the flailing light of that torch I had recognised that my assailant was wearing a policeman's summer blue shirt with shoulder tabs.

# *Two*

Generally speaking, I am a placid enough chap, though I've been told I'm too independent; but not, I think, aggressively so. One or two things make me wild, though. Such as the violation of personal property—and there are certain aspects of personal property that are unique and irreplaceable, the foremost of which, to a photographer, is his collection of negatives. They are what he lives by and for, and cannot be repeated. A fingerprint on one is pure outrage. So, to discover my files being tampered with was inflammatory, and I had every intention of getting out there again and tackling the villain. There was no thought of personal danger; wounds heal and skin replaces itself. But something had happened to my head, and I was in the dark. I could not work out which way was up.

Of course, as this was a darkroom the fastening was inside, so he couldn't lock me in, or even barricade the door with my pitiful collection of props as it opened inwards. So only my personal disability restrained me, that and the fact that when I did manage to open the door I was faced by another blank of darkness, he having closed the outer studio door. What with one thing and another, by the time I staggered out on to the landing he had gone.

I put on the studio lights and went back in. The top drawer was still open, so I could lean on it and try to assess my loss. The folder containing my negatives and the fifty-three proofs of the Ješić wedding had gone. Blood dripped on the folder relating to the job I'd done a month before for Darrow Engineering. I closed the drawer quickly before I did any more damage, and handed myself up the staircase to my living quarters.

The skin was broken behind my ear, but I stopped the bleeding with a plaster. The cat eyed my anger and distress from the draining board, and lamented with miserable yowls.

My folders are special wallets containing two pockets on one side for my proofs, and individual transparent sleeves the other, to hold strips of negatives. There is space for my personal records of time and date etc., and the exposures and films I'd used. I hadn't realised how convenient this would be for a thief; one grab and he had the lot. One thought obsessed me as I tidied myself, and that was to get them back. And, you see, I had a vague clue. One thing restrained me from driving off there and then to test it out; I'd thrown the petrol pump at his head.

Before I could go down and hunt it out I heard footsteps on my lower stairs, and then my buzzer went. I stuck my head over the top banister. A customer!

"I'll be right down."

"Are you Len Podmore?"

"Yes."

"Then we'll come up."

Two large men came, one behind the other, up my private stairs. This was another liberty. My temper was on the edge. I said: "Heh, hold on." They advanced without pause. I'd had my fill of big men, and looked

19

round for something heavy enough to even the odds.

"Police," said their leader, not in a reassuring voice but in a threatening one. I'd had my fill of coppers, too.

I went on looking, and I had my kitchen chair by its back when they shouldered through the door.

"What's this then?"

"You keep away from me."

"I am Detective Sergeant Keele, and this is my colleague, Constable Polly."

"Prove it."

"Now, now sir . . ."

"I've had enough of coppers."

"Got a record, have you?"

"I have not!"

Polly was watching this with placid interest. The sergeant turned to him and raised his eyebrows. "We got a right one here, Fred."

"We have that."

But they produced their little plastic authorities, with the passport-type photos of themselves. Being a specialist, I was just able to recognise them. I handed them back.

"Well all right."

"That's better, sir. Now can we all relax and have a few quiet words?"

He might've relaxed, I did not. It occurred to me that I was suddenly in a position to try out, and possibly strengthen, that clue I thought I had. So I attempted to give the impression of a man relaxing, whilst at the same time girding up my mental loins for a confrontation of intellect. That I was certain of success indicated my inexperience with the police. To me, this Sergeant Keele

20

seemed a bit thick, his brains being in his muscles. Certainly he had plenty of those and looked like a man who could walk through walls. He had a florid, round face and double chins, which he kept tucked well in, giving the impression of perpetually drawing back in dubious consideration.

I said: "Let's hear the few quiet words," and Polly wandered off across the room, ostensibly to gaze out of my window over the uninspiring roofs.

"Our information," said Keele, "is that you were the photographer at the wedding yesterday at St Godolph's."

I nodded. Keele scratched the side of his nose. "And it's occurred to my superiors that you may have seen something."

Polly glanced at him with a hint of amusement. I gathered that Keele did not normally admit to having superiors.

"I didn't see anything."

"But you were there at the time of the robbery?"

"So were hundreds of other people."

"But not with cameras."

"Ah!"

"What does *that* mean? Ah."

"Nothing. Just noticing the interest in my photographs."

"Who's interested?"

"The police, clearly."

He frowned. "You trying to be funny?"

"No. Just a bit surprised. With the crooks caught, and—"

"Who told you that?"

21

"It was on the radio."

His fat mouth gave a grimace. "If you mean by caught, dead."

"All three?" I was shocked.

"How d'you know there was three?"

"On the radio." That much I could say with confidence. But Polly was watching me with awakened interest. There must have been something in my expression.

"But you were surprised it was three," said Keele, so he had seen it too.

"Shocked." I looked from one to the other. "The radio said three men had been found at the scene of the car crash."

It's funny how your subconscious sorts these things out and files them. At the time, I had not consciously rejected the radio's report. But now it showed.

"But you thought there was something wrong with it," said Keele, very softly but in no way gently. As soft as the pad of a prowling panther. "You had a different figure in mind?"

I was sparring beyond my weight. "I'd assumed two. You know, in a car . . ."

"No, I don't. There're three in our car, the driver, Polly, and me." He casually lit a cigarette and blew smoke at the cat. He was now all confidence. "Where'd you hear two?"

"The radio," I suggested.

He glanced at my old long and mid-wave set. "Not on that. So—where?"

Then suddenly I knew where. I had a mental picture of dragging Martin Astel from the white Jag, and the patrol vehicle involved in the direct chase was reporting: ". . . car carrying two men now proceeding north along the by-pass . . ."

"I was passing a police car, and overheard . . ."

He cut me off with a loud, boisterous laugh. "You must have been moving fast. At around that time, every police car within fifty miles was racing to intercept."

I waved a hand vaguely. I was trapped. To mention the white Jag would involve the Ješićs, and I wanted a first go there. "Wherever it was . . ." I began. Then I had recourse to the only reaction available. I went on angrily: "Damn it, you must know. Two or three."

"There were two men in the car."

"So the local radio was wrong. Don't blame me."

"But there were three dead men at the scene of the crash."

"So where did the third come from?" I demanded, almost as though I had a right to know.

"You tell us. You seem to know all about it. Too much."

They waited. The silence pressed in on me. I fought against it. "I don't know why it's so important, when you got the money back."

"It's important because a bank cashier is dead."

"I didn't know that."

"Something you didn't know?" And yet, I felt I'd made a point. I genuinely did not know. "That and the fact that we did not recover the money," he conceded.

"You didn't?"

I suppose I'm no actor, and to get past an experienced policeman's interrogation you need to be perfect. That I had no expertise in this seemed to carry some weight. My confusion enforced my honesty. Keele shrugged, and his expression as he looked across at Polly was eloquent. All they had to deal with was a fool. I felt myself flush with anger, and yet at the same time hide behind the naivety of it.

"A funny lot of coppers you've got around here!" I burst out. "Four murders and a hundred and eighty thousand quid missing, and all you've got to do is come round and play games with me. What's the use of asking *me* things, when you know all about it yourself?"

Now it pleased Keele to be amused by me. "Not what you know. Not what you saw or heard, whatever that was." He grinned. When he did this his top lip seemed to stick to his teeth. "It's what your camera saw."

"The bank wasn't in my frame. Not once."

"All the same . . ."

"But you'd be welcome to see them. Oh yes. Only I haven't got anything to show you."

"Nothing? Not developed yet?"

"It so happens that my negatives and proofs have been pinched."

"Well now . . ." His voice was mocking, but his eyes hard.

"I tell you, they've been pinched!"

He shook his head, reproving my procrastination. "Tut, tut!"

"Then what the hell d'you think this is?" I turned my head.

"It's a plaster."

"He belted me with a torch."

"When was this, sir?" The mental notebook produced.

"Half an hour ago."

"A torch in broad daylight?"

"It's dark in my studio. I blanked out the window, on purpose."

"So you didn't see your assailant?"

"You don't believe a word I say!"

"Oh, but we do. We understand your reluctance to show us your results."

"I am *not* reluctant. And I did see my assailant, as you call him. He was another of *your* bloody lot. A copper."

There was silence. Keele's eyes narrowed. He was believing me, and he didn't like it. He ran a thumb up and down behind his lapel. Polly made a slight movement. "The other one . . ." But Keele gestured angrily, and the constable was still.

"Let's get this straight." The panther prowled behind Keele's eyes. "A man in the dark struck you with a torch. But you say he's one of us. Why?"

"I got a glimpse of his shirt. A copper's blue shirt."

"A patrolman's?"

"I don't know about that."

"Show us."

"Show you—what?"

"Where they were, these negatives and things. Where *he* was and how he stood." I looked from one to the other. "Now!" snapped Keele.

So I took them down to the studio, which was now as dark as I'd claimed. One of my light umbrellas still lay where I'd sent it plunging. The cabinet lock had been forced. I showed them the spots of my blood on the Darrow Engineering folder.

"Fingerprints?" asked Polly.

25

Keele glanced at him savagely. "You think?" Then at once he was pleasant, turning to me. "So you see, sir, you must have got something interesting."

"I'm glad of that. You might work up a bit of interest in getting them back for me."

"Oh, we're interested. Yes."

"So you'll try?"

"If they turn up, we'll let you know."

"Turn up?"

"During the investigation of a robbery involving four murders."

Which placed them firmly in their proper perspective. But perspective depends on viewpoint. For me, you could have their murders. What mattered to me was my negatives. Those primarily, because I could then re-print any amount of proofs. Frankly, I couldn't see them paying much attention to my paltry interests, even if the things did turn up. So I was less than helpful. There was something I could have done for them, but I failed to mention it.

They left. I rescued the petrol pump from a corner of the studio, and went down to replace it. This took a long time, because I wasn't concentrating, and the priming lever was bent.

What I was thinking about was that grinning copper, who had imposed himself in that early group. My first thoughts about him, before the arrival of Keele and Polly, had been that I had recorded a policeman who had been guilty of a dereliction of duty, in that he'd become involved with a wedding when he should have been on patrol with his mate. That he'd been prepared to rob my files in order to cover himself seemed rather like taking a sledgehammer to a peanut. In any event, his presence at the scene of the crime had been fortuitous, and surely it had been that car's chase which had led to the getaway car's capture, even though the crooks were dead and the money vanished. So, in that event, surely his slight lapse would have been excusable by his superiors. That had been my thought—until Keele appeared.

But now I knew more. There seemed to be a reluctance even to mention that patrol car, and if Keele had known of the officer involved—and how could they not be aware of the identity of the car that'd led them to the capture?—then he'd have known at once who had taken my wallet. Yet there'd been no hint that he did. Like that with the two other unexplained facts: the missing money and the third dead man. Link that third man with the driver of that patrol car, whom nobody had mentioned, and some very strange ideas began to emerge.

These ideas I was unable to face squarely; they were too vague. But they so obsessed me that I at first got the pump back wrong, with its lever the wrong side of its cam, and had to strip it off again. I was too busy assessing my single clue.

As I recalled it, the copper in my photo had indicated a personal interest in the Ješić wedding. If that were so, then they would know him. I had not told Keele this.

There was also a secondary consideration. A set of proofs were with Ruža and her family, another point I'd kept from Keele. I was pleased that I'd got them to the client so quickly, quicker than anyone could expect. Now, at least, they were available to me, whereas Keele, if he'd known, would surely have gone round there and impounded them. You see, from those proofs I could make copy negatives. They could not be as good as the originals. However careful and expert you might be, there's always a loss in quality. So I still wanted my originals, but copy negatives would be better than nothing, to go on with, and when I had them Keele was quite welcome to a set of prints from them.

When I had them! The way things were going with the car, it'd be midnight before I got away. The light was failing, the battery was dying, and I was in near-despair when the engine at last fired.

I left it running while I dashed back up for a quick clean-up, down again with my cameras in case any more intruders broke in, up again to leave some milk for the cat, then I clambered in and was off, with not a thought to a possibly tailing car. Inexperience again.

It was quite dark when I arrived at the Ješić's. In front of the house there was a squared drive, now very much potholed, which at one time had surrounded a lawn with shrubbery, perhaps. This had long since been worked into a flat patch of parking area, now scattered with about a dozen cars of assorted shapes and sizes. The clan Ješić was gathering, not, I hoped, to welcome me. Though, on second thoughts, the idea had vague attractions, if it could be assumed that the word had gone out to the four corners that the wedding photos had arrived. It was a diverting conceit, which I put behind me. I had not the slightest idea how to tackle this encounter, and could go on only one basic premise, that I would not be welcomed.

This thought was prompted by the general lowering aspect of the house. I had the feeling that I was watched. The Prefect was parked anonymously amongst the rest, butI felt that it stood out as though on fire.

I got out, locked it up, and went to the front door. I reached towards the bell-push, and the door opened, a slightly darker oblong against the unlighted porch.

"You should not have come."

It was Ruźa's voice, breathless, as though she'd run to prevent my ring.

"I had to see you."

A pause. "Me?"

"You and the others."

"Oh."

There was no light in the hall behind her. I said: "Something's happened. Can't I come in?"

"For a minute, perhaps."

She must have reached behind her. A dim light came on overhead. She was in a grey, slim dress, her eyes startled, her hair coal black.

"What is it?"

But I wanted to examine expressions and judge reactions. Not hers. Ruźa I felt I could trust, and so did not wish to bluff her.

"Where are they all?"

She gave a grand gesture, conveying the whole house, and seemed surprised at the question.

"Your father and mother," I amplified. "Your husband and his brother. The rest . . ."

"You'd better come through."

I felt that she had given way so as not to excite my suspicions. It made me even more suspicious. I followed her along the hall. Dimly, up above, I could hear music. Somewhere a child cried out with laughter.

"Ah!" said Poppa Jeśić, "the photographer."

"We've not really had time to examine—" began Ruźa, but I cut in.

"That's not why I came. I've had a burglary."

There were a dozen or fifteen people in the room. They viewed me with a languid patience.

"What was stolen?" Comus Astel asked.

I had always accepted Jeśić to be the patriarch of this group, but Astel's voice held a hint of authority. Nobody spoke as they waited for my reply.

"I'm afraid . . . the negatives, and my own proofs of the wedding."

"Only those?" Astel's eyes were quite calm. "Nothing else?"

"No." I was a bit annoyed. *Only* those!

"But you must have a lot of valuable equipment."

"Just the one wallet." I interrupted him.

Comus Astel was a big man, six-two probably, and with that delicate, almost fastidious economy of movement you often find in big men. There was strength in his face. "Him?" he asked, prompting.

"It was a policeman."

Silence again. Jeśić came forward, his arms loose, his head wagging. "A policeman stole your photographs?"

"So it seemed to me."

"And you come to us?"

"I thought maybe you'd know such a policeman."

It required an effort to come out with that. There was a tenseness in the air, a rustle of response. Sharply, a laugh cut through, bitten off. Jeśić glanced round amiably.

"Do we know any policemen?"

Then the atmosphere was dispersed with general

30

humour. Comus Astel allowed himself the hint of a smile. "You see, we can't help you in that."

"But there's another way you might."

"Anything . . ."

"Without my negatives I can't produce any prints, whatever anybody might want. So I'd like to borrow back the proofs I left here, and make copy negatives from them."

"Well now!" Ješić clapped his great, hairy hands together. "Ruźa—where are they?"

"All over."

"Then we must bring them together. Ljubica! You hear? Get moving, girl, and find the man's lovely pictures. Danny, you go with her. And hurry. We mustn't keep him waiting."

"No panic," I protested.

"Run, girl!" he cried, slapping her bottom as she danced past. She shrieked, and Danny Summers went with her. I gathered that sundry offshoots of the clan were dispersed throughout the house.

We waited. On their part, there was no awkwardness. They relaxed. Ješić seemed to be entertaining one group with a doubtful story of Yugoslavian origin, which required a vast amount of gesticulation and a dancing about on his clumsy feet. Momma Ješić laughed uproariously. There were cries for an encore.

Ruźa said: "I'm sorry you lost your negatives."

"I'll have copies."

"But it's not the same, I'm sure."

I loved her for appreciating that. "I'll get them back, never fear."

She glanced at me. "Do you think so?"

31

"I've only got to find that policeman."

"Oh yes . . . him."

Then Ljubica came back, shuffling a handful of prints, with Danny Summers at her heels.

"Here's some more," he said. "That's the lot." His laugh was infectious. I wondered if he was living there with Ljubica.

I skittered through them. "I make it fifty-one. There's two missing."

"Oh dear," said Ruźa. "Which two?"

"I'd have a job deciding that." Not exactly the truth, but after all we were swapping evasions, weren't we!

"I hope it's nothing that matters."

"It could, to you," I said. "That's the important thing."

She brightened. Her smile flashed. "I'm sure we'll be very pleased with what's left."

"That's all right, then."

"You're sure? I'd have worried if you'd been . . ." She stopped. Jeśić, his eyes everywhere, seemed to be listening.

"Been what?" I asked gently.

"Upset."

"I'm not upset," I told her, perfectly truthfully, because I'd proved something.

"Comus," said Jeśić, before it went too far, "show the gentleman out."

I was watching the shadow cross Ruźa's face when Comus touched my arm. No more than a touch. I turned. His eyes were grave. "This way."

We went silently to the front door. He opened it.

"Make your copies," he said. "Do a good job."

32

"Find me that policeman," I told him, "and I'll do a better."

I heard him laugh as I walked to the car.

# Three

I had not the slightest intention of making copies, because now I knew that the policeman was one of them. *They* had my negatives. I was determined to get them back, and my immediate intention was to return to the studio, spread the proofs out, and decide which were the two missing ones. With that knowledge I believed I'd have a lever with which to prise free my originals. You can see, I was becoming obsessed.

In such a way a child plays with matches.

I pulled out into the main road. A car parked on the opposite side, two hundred yards away, flashed its heads at me. I flashed back. He did it again. When I came closer I saw that he had his hand out of the window, waving me down. I drew in, nose to nose, and we cut our lights. I got out, and Sergeant Keele threw his passenger's door open in invitation. I climbed in and shut it behind me.

"What the hell're you playing at?" he demanded.

"Going about my lawful business. I've been to tell my clients that the wedding negatives have been stolen. They've got a right to know."

The proofs nestled snugly in the zipped pocket of my denim jacket.

He ran his palm gently, sensuously, around the rim of his steering wheel.

"And I bet they were interested," he said sarcastically.

I found this offensive. "They expressed polite concern."

He slapped the wheel and guffawed coarsely. "They were leading you on."

"Not a bit of it."

"They saw you for what you are."

"And what's that?"

"A bit of a mug."

I had the door half open. He put a hand on my arm. The fingers were claws. "Hold it." I paused. "Shut the door and listen."

I shut the door. "There's nothing I want to listen to."

"I've been thinking. You'd done your negatives and one set of proofs. *Your* proofs. I was slow. Of course, you'd do two sets, one for them and one for yourself. So you'd head for your client to borrow 'em back. Oh, I was slow . . . and you were playing cute with me, sonny."

I was perhaps ten years younger than him, and resented the condescension. I was wondering why he'd come out on this alone.

"Self-protection," I murmured.

He spread his palms, looking amazed. "From me?"

"You'd have impounded them, and I wanted copies first."

"So . . . hand 'em over. And I'll impound them now." He laughed again. His eyes, catching the light of a streetlamp, were unpleasant.

I drew the thick pack from my pocket. "Ah!" he said, and held them tilted away from him, to get the benefit of the same lamp.

I waited. He whistled softly. They flicked quickly beneath his gambler's fingers. "My, my," he said, his voice hoarse when he kept it low. "A right rogue's gallery you've got here."

"That's ridiculous."

"I can match thirteen of these faces from our police files."

"They are quite normal, reasonable people," I said distantly, wondering why I should trouble to defend them.

"What d'you expect, you clown, fangs and staring eyes? A shifty look? Of course they're ordinary, otherwise they'd be inside. It's why they're still free, by being ordinary."

Ruźa's eyes haunted me. "I can't believe that."

"Want to come down to the station? I'll show you."

But to see her face on a police photo would be more than I could take. "No, no. But all the same . . ."

"What cars did they use? For the wedding, I mean."

"Well . . . two Jags, one white, a maroon Daimler. An ancient Rolls. I don't know what else."

He flicked a switch on his dash and a red light shone. He spoke into his mike, a jumble of code recognition and response. At the end of that: "Stolen vehicles yesterday in a twenty-mile radius, please," he requested.

A short wait. Then the loudspeaker crackled. A list—heavens, I never thought there could be so many in one day—and:

"Daimler, maroon, ZJK427M; Jag, white, PHJ193S; Jag, green, LJW525K; Rolls, black, UK493, vintage . . ."

Keele snapped it off. "All recovered, abandoned. The Rolls was taken from an exhibition at Sutton Park. The white Jag . . ." His voice fell. ". . . is the Chief Superintendent's, taken from his drive."

36

I laughed.

"It's not funny."

But I knew the type of crooks I was dealing with. "It's not theft when they get it back."

"It's a bloody capital crime when it's the Chief Super's."

"Aren't we taking this too seriously?"

He groaned. "*You* are taking your negatives seriously. *I* am taking four murders and a robbery seriously. That's the difference."

"Them? It can't be. You're crazy, Sergeant. They were at a wedding."

"They're *always* at a soddin' wedding. Now get out of here and go home, and forget it."

"My proofs."

"I'm impounding . . ."

"Let me copy them first. Sergeant . . . please! I'll let you have a set of prints. Honest. But they're all I've got."

He was looking at me, grinning. Then he wiped the back of his hand across his nose. "You don't get it, do you! They're not interested in wedding albums and fancy mounted photos. Don't you understand?"

The grinning oaf! I set my teeth. "I took the pictures. They're my negatives, and I want 'em back."

He considered me, missing the point. I was pleading for a chance to take copy negatives, but what I really wanted was the originals. He couldn't know that I expected the one to lead me to the other.

"How long does it take?" he asked suspiciously.

"Two hours to take the new negatives. All night before I've got a new set of prints . . ."

"I'll give you the two hours. These . . ." He waved a

37

fistful of proofs. ". . . will do for me."

So I'd have no time for care, for the re-check and the second go with any that came out not too good. The copies were going to be even poorer than I'd thought.

"All right."

"I'll sit and watch."

You can see how far he trusted me. I followed him back to the studio, and we parked at the kerb. Duke Street was quiet at that time.

I used the Hasselblad on my enlarger stand, the proofs in the base frame, and two spots, one from each side. Once you get it right it's one every two minutes or so, with a break to change the film. Or films. Fifty-one shots on 120 film is five films.

"That it?" he asked wearily. No staying-power, these coppers.

"I'd have liked to develop them and check . . ."

"To hell with that. I got a woman waiting. Good luck to you, buster . . . and, one tip. Wait till they contact you. Okay?"

He went. The cat emerged from behind the drying cupboard. "Let's have a pot of tea," I said, and we went upstairs to get it.

The time was ten-thirty. I didn't really need those prints, I told myself. But yes I did. I wanted a set to thrust beneath Ješić's nose. Ones with the four cars on.

I took the tea tray back to the darkroom and loaded the spools. Ever tried reaching for a cup of tea in complete darkness? You can tell a photographer by that—he gets to memorise positions.

The negatives seemed good. Once again I felt a surge of pride. I hung them in the drying cupboard, went upstairs, set the alarm, and got an hour in.

Then we went downstairs and ran off a set of prints. Fifty-one of them. Only one set this time, for two reasons. One was that I was about dead on my feet, my eyes like clams covered with sand. The other was that I needed these only for one purpose, to force Ješić's hand. What I now considered to be my own set were now in the keeping of Sergeant Keele.

And besides, I knew, long before, which were the missing two: the shot of the groom and his best man entering the gate, and the group shot which had included the fake policeman.

It was obvious by then that he'd been a fake, which of course meant that the driver of the police patrol car in the background was also a fake. Which made the car itself . . . what?

My intention was to get myself round to the Ješićs' as early as possible, but when I got back upstairs the light was breaking over my spectacular roofs, and the cat had long since taken to my bed, so I joined him. It was eleven-thirty when I woke, feeling like death and fit to crawl under the carpet.

I had two days of beard to scrape off, and a rather mournful face to contemplate while I did it. Then, a quick soak, and I felt better. My muscles flexed themselves and prepared for action. My brain was like a bagful of bees.

Before I left I dug out the Darrow Engineering file and confirmed what I'd remembered. It was as I'd thought. Next door to the factory there was a car body repair workshop. I felt a little more confident.

They were having lunch. This was in the kitchen,

designed by Victorian standards to seat the staff, which, judging by the size of the house, would have been numerous. There were nineteen at the long table, Ješić at the head, Momma at the other end.

"Ah, the photographer!" Ješić said the same thing as before, but with even less enthusiasm.

Danny had let me in. He'd already asked me if I'd eaten, and frankly I'd been able to face nothing more than cornflakes. There was an air of suppressed excitement about him, as though I were to be the meal and the Ješićs the lion.

"He's hungry," said Danny, and that minx Ljubica spoke up. "Sit here by me. Danny, you find another chair."

She wasn't unlike Ruža, though a bit of a tease I suspected. I sat. A plate of some sort of aromatic stew appeared before me. A glass was filled with Riesling, a different one, a little lighter than at the reception. I ate. I drank. Ljubica wasn't the only tease around there. I savoured the expentancy that ran behind their apparently idle chatter.

Ruža was the other side of the table, two up from me. Whenever I looked up her eyes were on me. I thought she was pleading for something. Pretending I knew what that was I sat back, replete, sipped at my re-filled glass, then leaned forward like a card-sharp and spread my prints in front of her along the centre of the table.

"Oh, you've brought them back. So soon!"

"Those are copies."

"I wouldn't have known," she said loyally, her eyes bright. Ješić leaned forward. I caught his eye.

"The police have got the others," I announced casually.

Forks were poised. Glasses were stilled. I drank, put down my glass, and looked around me with what I hoped was naive lack of understanding.

"Can't imagine why," I admitted. "But Sergeant Keele was very interested."

"Do I know this Keele person?" asked Ješić to the company.

Comus, a few yards down, leaned forward. "No reason why you should, Jovan. The man's C.I.D."

"Ah, the plain clothes gentleman." He waved grandly to me. "You were saying?"

I had hoped to have them fluttering by that time. But I was facing strong nerves.

"He seemed," I said, "to be particularly interested in the cars in the background. The two Jags, the Daimler, the Rolls."

Comus lifted his glass to me, his eyes mocking behind it.

"But I believe they've got them back now," I said, and Comus nodded gently. "They were found abandoned."

Ješić tugged at his moustache. "I shall never trust that firm again."

"Will you need the cars again?" I asked politely.

"Ljubic isn't married. The last of my chicks."

She offered me a cigarette. I shook my head, not willing to take my eyes from Ješić.

"You'll have difficulty with the white Jag. The Chief Super's put an armed guard on it."

We all laughed. The wine laughing for me. Comus got up from his seat and moved along the ranks. He put a hand on the back of my chair and his lips to my right ear. He was smiling.

"Better leave now."

I was abruptly furious. "No!" I turned. His eyes burned. But I had them now. We knew where we stood. I shrugged him off. It must have been the wine.

"I know," I said, "Which were the two missing proofs."

Comus snapped his fingers in exasperation, and returned to his seat. Ruźa spoke quickly.

"I'm sure they can't matter."

"One is very important." I looked round. Dark eyes impaled me from all directions. "The groom and his best man arriving. Unique, that is, and the collection could be incomplete without it."

"We could manage," said Ruźa miserably.

"And the other . . ." I shrugged. "Just a group, but it's an early one, and though I can't remember the details I'm sure Comus was on that too." There was a sigh of exhaled breath. No mention of a policeman. "And as he isn't on any of the others—no, not one, I checked—then *that* one becomes important too."

"Comus is very shy," said Ruźa.

He looked about as shy as a rhino. "So you can see how concerned I am," I said. "I suppose they haven't turned up?"

Their blank faces indicated that this was wishful thinking. Jovan Ješić cleared his throat. He was not about to admit that wedding photographs were of very minor importance to him.

"We're all concerned," said Comus gravely.

Ljubica claimed that all the ones with her on had come

42

out a perfect delight.

"I'm sure you were equally delightful on that group we've lost," I assured her, and she squeezed my arm. Danny said he'd got something to do, and was half out of his chair when Ješić tapped the table. It was only a fingernail, but Danny relaxed. He looked worried, so I raised my eyebrows at him.

"So I thought," I said blandly, "seeing that we all agree how important they are . . ." I paused, challenging anybody to deny their importance. ". . . that we ought to stage a reconstruction. Two reconstructions." And my heart thumped as I threw out the blatant challenge.

Silence. Ješić looked down at his hairy hands. Ruźa seemed about to speak, then bit her lip.

"It shouldn't be difficult," I went on, strengthened by the silence, "though we'll have to do without the Daimler in the background. I assume? I suppose . . ." I left it hanging. Nobody offered to acquire the Daimler again. "So it'll just be a matter of getting everybody together again. Bride and groom, best man, mother and father, bridesmaids . . . weren't there a couple of relatives of the groom? Still, you'll know, and seeing that nobody seems to have anything better to do . . . shall we say tomorrow morning? The weather forecast is good, and provided we don't bump into another wedding we'll do fine. Agreed? Shall we say it's laid on?"

I paused. Looked at my empty glass and sighed. Waited.

I'd thrown it on the table under their noses. They could refuse. As an ordinary family group they could well have rejected the inconvenience, but the challenge

43

was there, and I'd left Ješić with the choice, whether to go along with me in a jovial manner—pandering to my artistic peculiarities—or refuse, and leave us both knowing why. I prodded at him.

"Though I haven't seen the groom around," I remarked, scanning the table.

Ruža covered her mouth. Momma reached over and touched her arm. Comus spoke harshly along the table.

"We'll discuss this, you and me together. Somewhere else."

The warning was there in his voice. It took all I had in reserve to face him.

"But everybody's here. Come on, it'd be a bit of fun. Just imagine if the vicar's around. He'll think he's seeing double." I couldn't quite manage the laugh I should have capped it with.

Jovan Ješić raised his eyes. "I think we might accommodate you in this. Though there are one or two details . . ." He coughed, and let it rest at that.

Somewhere in that house, I was convinced, was my wallet of negatives and proofs, and the two missing prints. They could have satisfied me in a minute, by faking a search and producing *something*. Look what we've found! Well now . . . And they knew I'd then go away satisfied. But no, they had to carry it on. Somewhere in that house was also, possibly, a hundred and eighty thousand pounds, and they were not about to initiate any searches.

"I'll attend to the details," I said confidently. "We'll have to have everything exactly the same, a police patrol car out in the street—"

Comus was on his feet. There was a rustle of expectancy. Ruźa's eyes were pleading.

"We'll settle the details," said Comus. "Outside."

A hand under my elbow was signalling me to my feet. Ljubica whispered: "Do as he says."

Jovan Ješić thumped the table with his fist. "No one rises before Momma."

We waited. She rose sedately. Jovan took her arm. They headed for the door. Comus was along the table in a flash, his fingers in my shoulder. "Out!" I was alarmed, and angry.

"Don't worry." I raised my voice above the sudden clamour. Ješić and his wife paused at the door. "Don't worry about the police car, I'll lay that on." But Ješić did not look round. The door closed behind them and there was a brief moment of suspended violence.

I stumbled under Comus's grip. I wasn't sure whether he was eager to get me from there because he cherished my safety, or because he couldn't afford the giveaway that the violence would mean. We were at the door. It was open. Momma and Poppa Ješić were five stairs up the grand staircase. I raised my voice. I'd kept the major challenge until last.

"And don't forget the copper. We'll need him for the group."

Comus slammed the door behind him. The Ješićs had not paused. He ran me towards the front door.

"What the hell're you trying to do?"

"I know it's a bit unconventional, but as a photographer . . ."

"Photographer?" His laugh was derisive. "Don't kid me."

"If you're not satisfied with my work . . ." All dignity,

45

insofar as my urged progress would allow.

"By God, you never give up, do you! Who d'you think you're fooling, feller?"

This completely undermined my confidence. There I was, attempting to force them into admitting that they were not as they seemed, and now I found that they did not believe that I was what I seemed. I stood out in the drive. His grin was sour.

"I'll let you know when I've got a police car." My major obstacle, tossed in as a token of good faith.

It only made him laugh. "Oh, you'll do that easy enough."

And the door closed. I felt like kicking something. Talk about calling bluffs!

That Comus Astel would take some watching, I decided, then I went and kicked my offside front tyre, and realised bitterly that I'd committed myself.

The blasted car started first touch. It would, when there was nowhere I wanted to go.

# Four

But I had a choice of two, equally unattractive. Either go looking for a police patrol car I could steal, or go home, kick the cat, and try to catch up on my sleep. So I drove to Darrow Engineering.

Darrow's had given me my best commission to date, two whole days around their factory, recording every stage of their production for a glossy hand-out their new Sales Manager wanted. No expense spared. They made fork-lift trucks, and one of my shots had been of a ranked row of trucks out in the dispersal area, awaiting delivery. I had based all my confident claims at the Ješić's on my memory of that time, and there was going to be no sleep until I'd done some confirming.

A photographer develops a special eye. His memory is of what is in his frame. On that he concentrates, and sometimes it is possible to recall a shot in full detail. What I had recalled was the side chain-link fence to the factory, where it abutted on to the next firm's property. I recalled crashed cars—these were recorded in the proofs on my files—but what was not recorded, and which lay only in my eye's memory, was the fact that a battered police car had been the other side of that fence.

So I drove along there to confirm it, and that, after three months, police cars were still being taken in by that firm. If not, I was sunk.

They described themselves as Casualty Body Repairs

Ltd. I parked out in the street. My car was in such condition that I could readily be accepted as a prospective customer, surveying the prospects. They had a long, low building smelling of spray paint, and a yard-full of dented vehicles. That was fine. All the cars seemed capable of moving under their own power, the only damage being to their bodywork. So far, so good. I edged along the kerb. I got out and had a closer look. Tucked away, as though they could take their turn if and when, were three police cars, one duck-egg blue with a white stripe, which didn't interest me, and two white with a red stripe, edged in blue, which did. My heart beat faster. Both were a bit inaccessible, but were parked along the far fence, beyond which was a large vacant expanse of pocked wasteland. The main gate was large and heavy, and obviously intended to be securely padlocked at night. But I wasn't going to be interested in gates.

I drove home. The cat went unkicked. My intention now was sleep, but two jobs turned up unexpectedly, a passport and a local actor wanting hand-out portraits, and obviously aiming for the big time, though he was going to be disappointed when he saw his profile. I dozed in my easy chair from six onwards, and the cat went out looking for a mate. Which I'd have been better doing.

Darkness comes late in June. It had to be one of those bright, clear nights, of course, the air still, the visibility about ten miles. What happened to that lovely smog we used to have? It was eleven-thirty when I tucked the Prefect into a corner of Darrow's car park, which was outside the factory to keep the inside roadways clear. All was quiet. My plastic heels seemed to echo into the distance. Something dark and furry ran from me across the wasteland.

I should have noted the streetlamps. One threw all its light along the side fence of Casualty Body Repairs Ltd, so it was going to mean the rear. Ah well!

I felt better back there, shielded from the road by the bulk of their long shed and all the wrecked vehicles. In my left hand I was carrying a large pair of wire cutters, but I might have guessed that the local junior gangsters would have surveyed the situation. There was a gap near the ground, which would have admitted a ten-year old. With a bit of persuasion it accepted a twenty-six-year old.

I stood inside. The moon threw my shadow at my feet. It seemed to shimmer. At around that time I decided to abandon the project. Then I recalled Comus's remarks, and moved ahead.

It was clear that my choice of police car was limited to one. The other white one was so boxed in that I'd have had to move a dozen other vehicles to get it out. Even this one didn't have a clear run. I'd be scraping its paint! I heard myself giggling at the thought, and abruptly stood still, taking one deep breath and a couple of swallows. I had clearly come unprepared.

One or two things I didn't know. Would it run? The damage could well be more than skin deep. And would it, if runnable, have petrol in the tank? And one other thing—would its door open to my convenient touch? I'd got a length of wire to short out the ignition, and I'd studied my own coil lay-out to decide how to do it, but if the door was locked I'd be sunk.

I approached it. The moon preceded me. I stopped. I

dropped the cutters. The damage to this one was a buckled near-side wing. The rust stood out black in the moonlight. And I recognised it, with bitter, heart-stopping certainty. That missing shot of the groom and best man returned to me with piercing clarity. This was the same patrol car that had parked outside the church gate.

For some reason I wanted to run. Superstition, no doubt. Then I could have cried out with joy. This was ideal. The very same car! Oh yes, we could reconstruct the scene well enough. We could do it down to the finest detail.

I approached. Now I was confident. Nothing was going to stand in my way. The thought of presenting this specific car to the Ješićs was irresistible. And the door was un-locked. By heaven, open, the driver's side. I slid in. Where did the Marina keep its bonnet-locking catch?

With the movement of the car on its springs, a bulk stirred in the seat beside me. I glanced sideways. The moon glinted on a medallion. It picked out the spots of a treble row of beads. It shone green on the thin, sallow dead face of Martin Astel before he slumped forward from the seat.

The steering wheel was hard in my chest. There didn't seem to be enough air. I gasped for it. The cutters clattered at my feet, and I left them there, diving out of the car on hands and knees, scrambling away towards the fence. The mesh caught at my panic and clasped me like a copper's fist. I fought my way clear, and staggered over the rough ground out into the open and away from there. And stopped.

Think, Len, think. What the hell are you doing? Where heading? Home and tuck your head in, and throw it all away? It was too late to turn back. I had discovered a dead body. There was only one thing to do; I had to report it to the police. It was a citizen's duty.

I hunted shadows back to my car. I sat and thought about my duty as a citizen, and realised I was going to have a hell of a lot of explaining to do regarding that particular body. Perhaps skulking at home would be the best course, or an anonymous phone call. Blessed anonymity—with my bloody fingerprints on the cutters in the car!

There was perhaps only one person who would understand my predicament—understand, not sympathise with. That was Sergeant Keele. I started the engine, and gently, so as not to be picked up for speeding, went on a search for a phone box.

I had completely forgotten that it was around midnight. 999 gets you the station, but not the C.I.D. officers, unless they're on a special job. Such as murder.

"He'll be at home, sir. If you could just tell me . . ."

"It's got to be him."

"In the morning, perhaps."

"It's important."

"Perhaps I could get him to call you back. If you'll give me your name and number . . ."

But I knew that one. They'd have a car round in a couple of minutes, and have me inside for a grilling.

"Give me his home number."

"He wouldn't be pleased."

"I could try all the Keeles in the book." An empty claim, there being no book in this half-wrecked box.

"He's ex-directory, sir."

It went on like that for a few more minutes. A phone

box can become very hot indeed. I imagined them tracing the call . . . Then at last I got the number, thanked him, and recalled that I'd emptied my pockets of change before coming out, so as to obviate any stray tinkle during my illegal activities.

I asked the operator to ask Keele if he'd accept the call, and pay for it. That, I think, was my mistake. He wasn't pleased.

But by the time we were speaking together he was certainly wide awake.

"Podmore! What the hell . . ."

"Listen. It's important."

"It's bloody midnight. What're you doing wandering round loose at this time?"

The detective's mind. He'd know I was calling from somewhere other than my own phone.

"Let me explain."

"Don't tell me—don't you dare tell me you've dug me out at this time to talk about your bleeding negatives!"

Not *my* negatives, *his* corpse. A sense of outrage overcame me. "It's something to do with that. If you'd just let me tell you . . ."

"I'll kill you. So help me . . . Heh, you're not at the Ješić's? If you are . . ."

"I'm not there."

"Then you've *been* there."

"I have been there. But I'm not there now."

"I warned you," he shouted. "Didn't I warn you to keep away from them? But you had to be clever. Oh, don't come crying to me . . ."

"I'm not crying." Only nearly screaming in an attempt to get through.

"They're crooks. Didn't I make that clear? We've been after 'em for years. Always pull the same trick, and it always works. A church by a bank—you listening to me?"

"I'm listening," I whispered.

"A church by a bank, and a quick raid on the cashier's during the ceremony. The loot chucked into the bride's car, and half the time some dumb copper clearing the way for them through the crowds. Seven soddin' times that I know to."

"Seven," I whispered.

"They're not interested in your pictures. You were just background, mate, to make it look good. Why'd they want your stuff? That Ruźa, she'd be knee-deep in wedding shots. She's been married seven times in the past three years. And that's just the ones I know. Did you say something?"

I'd coughed. It was that or be sick. I shook my head— no, I hadn't said anything.

"And sometimes, friend," he said, almost gleefully imagining my distress, "They pinch a police car, and use it to draw off the pack. *That's* the crowd you've got in with, that's the lot you're pestering for bloody negatives. Go home, son, go home and stick your head under the pillow. They'll be gone in a few days—if we don't get a line on 'em before." He paused. "You hear me?"

I croaked: "I hear you," and hung up halfway through his next sentence.

I managed to get to my car. I sat. I thumped the steering wheel a few times. Then gradually the nausea gave way to fury. Seven times! It wasn't illegal, marrying seven times in three years, not if the previous ones were dead. So . . . scattered around the countryside were the corpses of six previous husbands of Ruža Ješić, she of the brown eyes speckled with gold and the skin tone I'd reached for. I felt the touch of her fingers on my arm, and I shrugged them off with anger.

Fear, ecstasy, misery can all stifle completely a person's normal reactions. Fury can do it too. I think that if I had been less angry I couldn't have done what I did next. If it had not remained with me, like a cloak, I could not have continued with it.

I drove back to Darrow's and parked in the same corner. I returned to the rear of Casualty Body Repairs, contemptuous of concealment. The area was mainly industrial. No one and nothing restrained me. I crawled again beneath the fence and marched purposefully to the car, yanked open its door, and fumbled around for my cutters. My face was close to Martin Astel's. We could have whispered together, of revenge and retribution. There was a dark hole in the centre of his forehead.

I cut a large gap in the fence. The moon was lowering. I returned to the car and got the bonnet open, attached my wire, using the torch I found in the glove compartment. It started. I bounced it out of the gap, and vented some of my anger on the suspension, forcing it over the rough territory. Then I was out on the road, and driving like all hell for the Ješić house. I'd have used the winking light only it was covered by a black nightgown thing. The siren switch I could not find. That was a pity. I'd have enjoyed driving up with everything going, and dumping myself in front of their door.

But I had the horn ring. I put my hand on it and left it there until lights bounced against the upper windows and sashes slammed up. Then I got out, and stood in the fan of the full headlights.

"I've got the bloody car," I shouted. "Now show me your copper."

# Five

Somebody opened the front door, otherwise I would have battered myself to death against it.

The hall was huge. Some of them had reached the floor and were scattered about in pyjamas and night-dresses and dressing gowns. The Ješićs were halfway down the staircase. Comus Astel was at my right elbow, so perhaps it was he who had let me in. I didn't thank him. My anger was on the boil.

"All right!" I shouted, looking round at their startled faces. "I told you I'd get a police car. Well . . . there it is outside."

Comus caught hold of my elbow. "Don't you know the time! You gone crazy or something?"

I shook him off furiously. He drew back a fist, but hesitated when I glared at him.

"So you just get the rest of it ready," I challenged. "The people. Or are you going to be in trouble there?"

Nobody spoke. Ješić raised a hand from the bannister in despair, then put it down again. Ruža had her arm against the wall, supporting herself. Tiny teeth shone between her lips.

"What about that copper?" I demanded. "Have you got him for me?" I stared round them, making an exaggeration of it. "Oh, what lovely blankness! I've got a whole rep company here. The policeman! Remember? The one from the car. He's one of you—I bet he's here in the house. You must think I'm stupid. It was obvious, as soon as I knew which proofs had been pinched. Why take the negatives and my proofs, and those particular two? That's what I asked myself. Because they had the same thing on them, that's why. Police. Fuzz. *That* was what was common. The police car on one and the copper on the other. Go on, look all amazed. Or are you all admiring my reasoning? But I know now. I couldn't see how it worked in, but now I've found out a few things. He was one of yours. It's been done before. A police car to draw the action in the wrong direction. Oh, very cute. Very clever. But this time somebody'd got it on film. How very annoying for you. Go on, somebody deny it. Tell me I'm imagining things. But the real police don't use battered cars, and that one was. It bloody-well was, and to prove it I've got the same one outside. Go on . . . go and have a look."

Just try saying all that on a hot peak of fury. Try saying it to a dozen or so unresponsive faces, and see how you get on. I was faltering. My throat was harsh with the pressure of my anger, and my voice was failing.

"Somebody get him a drink," said Ješić kindly.

"Keep your drinks!"

"No, I'll deal with him," Comus put in, and I realised that he, of them all, was the only one fully dressed.

"Oh, you can deal with me well enough, I'm quite aware of that. But you're going to listen first. Then you'll know how much there is to be silenced." Brave words. I felt like death, anyway.

Slowing down by that time, though. I had relapsed into a calmer and more intense mood, one soaked in despair and disgust. Ruźa I barely dared glance at, but I

57

knew she had lowered herself on to a chest, her pretty nightdress spread around her.

"I know how it was done," I said. "Weddings are sweetness and light. Bank robberies are vicious aggression. Nobody links the two. So you plan a job and a wedding. You use the wedding cars—and even *them* pinched!—to get the takings away. And how nicely the police wave you through! Then the heavies get away in their vehicles, with the fake police car drawing the chase in another direction. You must be proud."

"All right Len," said Comus, using my christian name for the first time. "That's enough."

But I was getting no reaction. Nobody protested, nobody shouted at me angrily. Ljubica, seated on the bottom stair, bit her thumb and displayed her bottom, and Ruźa's eyes were wide and moist. My anger resparked.

"But I don't care about the money. I'm not one of your upright citizens. I'm dead selfish. I want my negatives. Keep your money, but give me what's mine. Then I'll go away, and do you the most splendid album you've ever seen. Hell—what'll it be? Number seven or number eight? There must be a whole trunkful of wedding albums. But you can have mine for nothing. There's a bargain for you. What d'you say?"

They said nothing. Ruźa sobbed. Momma Ješić slowly sank, her hand supporting her on the banister, until she sat on a high stair. Ješić clenched his fist and thumped his head.

If they'd said anything—if they'd drawn weapons and mowed me down with bullets—I could have taken it. But nothing ever stirred them. They had not responded to my earlier bluff, and this was no bluff. But . . . nothing. I was emotionally caught in a whirlwind, and they didn't even feel the draught. Damn it, I was pleading for help. I was close to sobbing when I went on.

"Or do we have to go through with the reconstruction after all? We'll do it. I'll go that far. At least I'll come face to face with your copper. But say something. Help me. I don't know where to go from here."

Nothing. No response. They waited to see how far I'd take it.

"Don't make me say it," I pleaded.

There was a pain in my chest. I lifted my head, and at last Jovan Ješić spoke.

"Say it. Let's hear all you think you know."

If there hadn't been contempt in his voice . . . I felt hot.

"No offers! No compromise! Oh, you're hard. How does anybody talk to you lot? Aren't you human? How many weddings have you had?" And like a fool I had to look directly at Ruźa just then. Worse, I couldn't take my eyes from her as I went on.

"Seven, has it been? Keele knew of seven. Seven husbands. And what happened to them? Say it, Ruźa. Say you'll agree to the reconstruction. But you can't, you can't. Christ!"

Despair then, my voice breaking. Her lips were apart, but she didn't find any words. The matt olive of her skin was a dirty green.

"But you can't do it, can you Ruźa! This husband, too, he's gone the way of the others. For pity's sake . . . did you have to kill them all?"

She was drawing in a great, tense breath. I shouted:

59

"I've got him outside. Brought him back for you. Only he's got . . . a hole . . . in his head."

Then she screamed. I moved. I had to stop that scream, but Comus was in front of me, murder in his eyes, and he slapped me so hard across the face that my mouth split against my teeth. There were shouts, and Ljubica was spitting angry words into my face. The screams went on. Somebody had my arm, otherwise I would have fallen. I was aware of a rush past me out on to the drive.

Suddenly the car's headlights went out and all the reflected illumination disappeared. I was thrust outside and the front door slammed. The screams that had been hammering at me were cut off. Comus whirled me to face him. He caught my chin in his hard hand. His face was stiff.

Only the upstairs light caught his expression.

"No!" My blood spattered his face.

"They're going to tear you apart."

"It wasn't me killed him."

"But you brought him here. And we all love Ruźa."

"You killed her husband . . ."

"Don't be a blasted fool."

Something was wrong. With my head steadying from his slap and the cool night air on my face, I knew something was wrong. Why should Ruźa be so upset at the death of this husband, if she'd lost half a dozen or so before? And Comus was Martin's brother!

I licked my lips. They tasted salt. "I can't run."

He jerked open the door of a Landrover. "Then get in my car. And sit quiet."

I couldn't understand why he was prepared to help me. Perhaps they couldn't deal with too many corpses at the same time. I slumped down in the seat, my eyes just above the sill.

They had the car's door open. Danny Summers was looking back at Comus. I heard what he said. "It's your brother right enough."

Comus thrust them aside. He crouched, and lifted Martin's head. I wondered, then, about the limpness of the body, having heard something about *rigor mortis*. But I know now that it wears off. Martin had been dead for two days. Comus was looking intently at the black hole in his brother's forehead, then he lowered his head gently, got to his feet, and shut the car door.

"Get back in the house." His voice was empty.

"What're you going to do?" they asked.

"I'll deal with it. Get inside. I want those lights off."

He waited. He had the authority. They left him alone with the car, and he waited until all the upstairs lights had gone out. Then he came across to the Landrover and got inside beside me.

How do gangsters bury their dead? Do they claim them from the police? I said: "What're you going to do?" I really meant with me.

"You're going to take him back where you found him. Then—an anonymous phone call . . ."

"Not me."

"You will, after I've told you the truth of it."

"That," I said, "will be a change."

"Oh, don't sound so damned smug. You haven't made a very good showing. All glib with your theories, but you didn't give it time. You didn't think it through."

"I'm not a detective."

"Then don't try to act like one. You're not even

basically logical. We're in the bank business. We're not murderers."

For some reason I was shivering. "Ain't it murder, then, killing a bank clerk? Or is that all part of the game?"

"That wasn't us, you fool. It happened too soon for us. We were all prepared. Ten minutes later, fifteen perhaps, and we'd have been in there. But they beat us to it."

"Easy to say." I coughed. "Do you have to smoke in here?"

He stubbed it out. "Easy to say, because it's true. You were dead right about the basic set-up, though. We had the cars laid on. The police car outside, that was ours, but we didn't get a chance to use it. Otherwise, and think about it, why should it have led the police *to* the gateway car? We always use it to lead them away."

He was very persuasive. His voice was even and without emphasis. He could be pleasant when he chose.

"You said—them. You're saying some other lot did the bank raid?"

"And we know who. Its got their mark. That was probably Quayle and Minnit in the bank, with Carraway at the entrance. They panic. It was a sawn-off that killed the cashier."

"Which you've never used, I suppose," I said in disgust. "You do these bank jobs with plastic guns, do you?"

His voice fell. I found it chilling. "There's never any reason for shots. Show anybody the bad end of a gun, even unloaded, and they do things. The big nothing at the end, oh it works wonders. But Quayle's nerves are in rags. They shot the cashier."

"You know it all, don't you!"

"Not all. Not yet. One or two things . . ." He shrugged. "That police car we'd laid on was outside the gate, waiting."

"For your fake copper?"

"For him. The driver's name was Petar Ješić. Ruźa's brother."

"Was?"

"Whoever got in that car with him . . ." His voice changed emphasis. "Petar was never a gunman. He wouldn't have known which end to hold. But he could drive. Lord, how he could drive! So, if you'd got in with him and stuck a gun in his ribs, he'd drive."

I was impatient. My mouth was swelling inside, my lip thick. "How many more have you got to tell me about? Your lot didn't do this, didn't do that. Not the bank job, and now not the car."

"Len, now listen. Take it easy. Quayle did the bank. The police car was ours, laid on, and we'd have used it if we'd had the chance. And we'd have done exactly what it did do, seeing that Quayle had jumped us to it. That's home-in the police on their getaway car. But that wasn't quite what happened. The police were shuffled around. They were kept at a distance by the radio in that police car—but not too much of a distance. Far enough away so that they never saw the getaway car forced off the road. And never saw the two men in it shot, and the money transferred to the police car. And Petar shot through the heart and dumped in a ditch. *Then* the police got the position, and when they got there the patrol car was gone."

63

I sat breathless. Ruźa's brother . . .

"Two double-crosses," said Comus softly.

"Two? I don't understand."

He barked a short laugh. "What you don't understand'd fill a book. Two, Len. One: The tip-off to Quayle, so that he could get in first. Two: the tip-off to somebody else, to cut Quayle out and bag the money. Two double-crosses . . . and *you* have to come round with your bleating about negatives and reconstructions!"

Almost, he made me feel ashamed. "Things are bad?"

"We'd been doing too well. It had to come to an end."

"Like this? Murder and robbery and . . . your brother. The last," and now I was asking, "of a series of husbands?"

He lit another cigarette, not thinking. I said nothing.

"Martin and Ruźa," he said gently, containing the emotion, "have been married seven times. It's not illegal, you know. Seven blessings, that's all it amounts to. It wasn't necessary to find seven different bridegrooms. And it would've been messy." Again that short, bitter laugh. I felt small. "But Martin was getting nervous and restless. I could tell. I think it was Martin who betrayed us to Quayle. I think he went for his cut, and they shot him. I'm waiting . . ." He looked at his fingertips. "Waiting for a chance to meet Quayle."

"To ask him?"

"I don't think there'll be time for questions. Now, you see how we're fixed. I want you to drive Martin back to where you found him."

"I'd like to . . . can I see Ruźa first?"

"No. Get moving away from here. And never come near us again. Things are getting rough. Jovan wants to

64

head out for Beatings."

"Beatings?"

"Quayle's place in Gloucestershire. He prides himself on a sense of humour. But it's not the way. I'm fighting Jovan, but I may lose. So stay away."

"Why have you told me all this?"

"To stop your stupid, stubborn brain from ticking over." He tossed the cigarette out of the window. Smoke drifted from his nostrils. "So . . . get going."

"But you haven't stopped it. My brain, I mean."

"Now what?"

"I admit I was a bit too clever. All I thought about was what was common in those two missing prints, and I came up with your fake copper and the car you had waiting. But that was too simple."

"Leave it, man," he said impatiently.

"No. My negatives were pinched. There had to be a valid reason. I assumed it was your copper, getting them before the police took a look. But that wouldn't have achieved anything. No . . . listen."

He was angry. "I'm getting fed up with you. Shut it off."

"From what you say, the police weren't going to land this job on your lot. It wasn't your style — you said that — and the police go by that sort of thing. They know where to pick you all up, and they haven't made a move. So there was nothing on my photos to hide. Nothing that I've realised, anyway. So why were the two proofs deliberately lost? And *that* was somebody here, at the Ješićs', whoever might have pinched my negatives. So why? What's with those two prints that we haven't seen? Tell me that, then I'll go away happy."

"Happy or not, mate, you're going. I've got no answers for you, so stop thinking about it."

"Even if the answer leads to whoever climbed into that car with Petar Ješić and dumped him in a ditch?"

He slammed the door open. "Even then," he snapped. "Get going, and don't come back."

"I'm not making any promises."

He stood outside, breathing deeply. "Len Podmore," he said, spacing the words, "I've never yet had to load a gun. But by God, I'll load one for you, if that's what'll stop you thinking."

I climbed down on to the ground, not feeling steady. He came round and put a hand to my elbow, not to assist me but to make sure I headed for the police car. I hesitated. It was not a pleasant thought, getting back in there, though I hadn't worried coming there.

"Take him and leave him where you found him. That's not Martin in there, it's just the body he used to use."

I got in. The engine was still running, getting a bit hot.

"I'll see you again?"

He grimaced. "God willing, no."

Then I drove away.

Stop thinking, he had said, when my mind was racing with conjecture. Who the hell was *he* to tell me to stop thinking? Admitted he'd been somewhat sympathetic to me, and on the face of it had helped me, but I had no way of knowing how far I could accept his word.

So I drove, thinking about not thinking, and the presence of the body of Martin Astel did not concern me at all, because I had forgotten it was there.

Well, not quite forgotten, perhaps. On the way to the Ješićs' I had been so incensed that nothing but the shortest route would serve, which had meant driving straight through the centre of town. On my return I was a little more circumspect, and did a kind of loop. At two in the morning it was unlikely I'd cause much comment, but there was no sense in being rash. The trip, therefore, was about five miles, and as I was reasonably new to the district I got myself lost once or twice. I cannot therefore say exactly where I was when I first noticed the police patrol car on my tail.

As I've mentioned, I had a black plastic cover over my Police sign and the flashing winker. This, perhaps, was suspicious. In any event, they merely drifted along behind me, curious perhaps. Maybe they were busy on their radio, checking which car might be in their area. There was no traffic in which I could hide. I simply had to drive. Until my nerve went.

Suddenly I was in a panic. I decided to drop him. The Marina I was driving seemed to have had special work done on its engine, so that at first I was pleased with my tactics. But the Marina they were driving had similar characteristics, plus a driver who had been trained how to use them. The chase was short. They drew alongside and waved me in. In my rear-vision mirror appeared another patrol car. There seemed not much point in going on.

So I stopped, got out, and ran for it. This, too, was no use at all. The lads had been bored in the immensity of the night, and gave chase gleefully. They caught me in less than half a mile. They led me back.

"Now," said one of them. "Let's see what we've got here."

They saw.

Then they used their radio. Instructions were given, and in a procession of three—one of them taking over the Ješić car and the other guarding me—we headed for the station.

It was clear that my night had barely commenced.

# *Six*

For some time I sat alone in a small bare room with one table and three chairs. I tried all three in turn, but they were equally uncomfortable. It gave me time to think what I was going to say that would get me out of there, which was a pity, because I would have been healthier inside.

Eventually, two men came in to see me. One introduced himself as Detective Inspector Hinkley. The other was Sergeant Keele. Hinkley was a grave, spare man in his fifties, with grey at his temples and an air of weary disillusionment.

"Now tell me, Mr Podmore," he said, "how you came to be driving a police car with a man's body in it."

He had taken a seat opposite me, and he pushed across a pack of cigarettes. I believe they always do that. I shook my head.

"I don't smoke. The car? I was bringing it here."

"As it happens, you were heading the other way."

"Well, I'm a bit of a stranger around here. You see, I opened this photographic studio in Duke Street about three months ago . . ."

"But you were going the wrong way." He made it sound a kindness that he was keeping me on a firm line of enquiry.

"As I was explaining, I was lost." I decided to improve on it. "I'd have asked a policeman, but it was one of your cars, and I didn't want to get involved with a lot of stupid questions." Chatty, you understand. Man to man. I felt wide awake.

He glanced at Keele, who took the third chair and a cigarette from the pack. Keele seemed weary and a little defensive. I realised that he was probably recalling our telephone conversation.

"Well . . . now you are," said Hinkley, his mouth twisting. "Involved right up to the neck in stupid questions. So you lost your way. From where?"

"I'd found it, you see. This car. And as it had this dead person in it—his name is Martin Astel, by the way . . ."

"You know that? Not just a stray body you happened to come across? Not simply a murder you just sort of encountered at two in the morning while going about your innocent affairs?"

Like that, was it? "I know him. I took his photograph only a couple of days ago. At a wedding . . ."

The trouble with these sarcastic devils is that you bounce your remarks against their complete lack of reception, and it becomes more and more difficult to go on. He nodded when I paused.

"Go on. The wedding at St Godolph's, you're talking about."

"Sergeant Keele's told you."

"He doesn't need to tell me. I'm in charge of the investigation of that bank robbery. And of four murders. No, five now. I wonder if we've run out of murders yet. Or do you know of a few more bodies?"

Not off-hand I didn't. I shook my head. This, I realised, was going to be difficult. I fell back on his own brand of humour.

"I'll keep in touch."

"Oh, you will. Unless I get some very straight answers you'll be staying here, my friend. Within touching distance."

I'd gone too far. "It's the photographs, you see."

"I've heard about the photographs."

"I'd obviously got something on them that mattered, in some way or other. Otherwise, why did somebody pinch the lot? So I did a bit of thinking . . ."

"Thinking? What right have you to start thinking?"

"He's always doing it," said Keele in disgust.

"No . . . please," I tried. "A photographer gets so that he remembers what was in his shots, and I thought—"

"A photographic memory?" asked Hinkley with interest.

"Visual, anyway." He had seemed to relax, and was being jovial with me. I relaxed too—a mistake, that. "If I've taken a shot of a row of fork-lift trucks, for instance, I can get a mental image of that picture, and actually count how many there were. But ordinary numbers— hell, I can't even remember phone numbers."

"Get on with it," said Keele savagely, no doubt at the mention of phone numbers.

Hinkley moved the cigarette pack an inch or two with one finger. He kept his eyes down. "Let him tell it his own way," he said gently. "Podmore?" His eyes came up. They seemed to be contemplating the inside of my head.

"It's just that I remembered one of the shots at the wedding, one with a police car in the background, and the more I tried to remember it, the more convinced I was that it'd got a dent in it. A rusty great dent."

71

Wandering away from the truth there, but only reversing it a little. I swallowed, and he noticed my nervousness. "And I remembered a job I'd done for Darrow Engineering."

"This memory of yours working overtime," Hinkley commented. "Darrow, did you say?"

"Next door to a car—" began Keele.

"I know. We send all our body repairs there." He had not taken his eyes off me. "So you remembered Casualty Body Repairs, and you went along . . . No, you tell it. I wouldn't have the nerve to put it into words."

"If you already know what I'm going to say . . ."

"Your own words. And remember . . . if you're going to say you found the car *there*, remember that you were heading away from here and towards there when they picked you up."

They must have turned up the heating. A spot of sweat dripped from my nose. In agitation I picked up the cigarette pack and banged it on the table.

"I told you, I got lost."

"From Duke Street, where you live, you'd go past here to get to Darrow Engineering. If you got there, how come you couldn't find your way back?"

"I'm a stranger . . ."

"Having regard to the photographic memory of yours."

I cleared my throat. "I was a bit upset."

"Understandably. When you'd just found a dead body in a car."

"I'm glad you can see that."

"The disappointment of it, too," he said, his eyes wide, all sympathy.

"Not . . . exactly . . . disappointment."

"No? But surely you're about to tell me that you remembered dented police cars in the yard of Casualty Body Repairs, and you thought you'd go and check, although it was around midnight and nobody would be there. But you'd find your way in, you thought. Illegal entry that'd be. And check that the same car was there—this memory of yours . . . how very useful. And . . . no, I can't say it. Sergeant, finish it for me."

Keele, when he spoke, sounded dull and toneless. There was no enthusiasm in it. "Sir, he'd think that maybe his stolen negatives would be in it."

That, I admit, was the big snag in my prepared story, and put like that it sounded a bit bald. Why else would I be hunting for the car—why else that I could mention?

"It was a copper who pinched the damned things in the first place," I tried.

"So I've heard," said Hinkley sourly. "Not one of ours."

And he knew very well from whence that copper had come! I could see he did. He could see I saw it, and that I knew too.

"I've never heard such a blatantly fabricated story in all my years on the force," said Hinkley with sudden anger. "Why on earth should you expect the *same* car to be in for repair, and if you did, how could your blasted negatives have found their way into it?"

"If," I suggested miserably, "it'd been taken out, used . . . illegally, I suppose . . . used and . . . sort of returned."

"Oh, we've got a right one here," Hinkley exploded.

Keele nodded sagely. "So I've already observed,

73

Inspector." But the sergeant's eyes were wary.

"Well . . ." I looked from one to the other. "It was the same car outside the church. The patch was rusty, and you people wouldn't be using a car in that condition. So I reckoned—it must've been taken from a repair place somewhere, and this was the only one I knew . . ."

"Go on. Why've you stopped?"

But I'd remembered that the fence had been reasonably secure before my attack on it with the cutters.

"I don't know how," I admitted, and I felt completely beaten. "How it was taken and how it was returned."

"Something you don't know! You amaze me. But we haven't yet learned the tortuous mental process by which you decided your negatives might be in that car."

"Excuse me, Inspector. But really, it wasn't me who said that. It was him." I pointed to Keele.

"Then what *did* you expect?"

"Only a lead. I mean, the car wasn't in use by your people, because the policeman who pinched my negatives wasn't one of yours."

"I said that a minute ago. You didn't know it before."

"I reckoned. Guessed. I was looking for a clue."

"A clue, indeed! What right have you to go ferreting for clues?"

"I want my negatives back."

"Your paltry, damned stupid wedding pictures . . ."

"Excuse me, but they're mine. Clues might be yours, but photographs are mine."

Hinkley blew his breath out, fluttering his lips. I said:

"But I honestly didn't expect to find Martin Astel in the car."

"Yet, having found him, you calmly proceeded to

74

demolish half the fence in order to bring him here, and finished up driving him *back*."

"I got lost," I whispered. So they'd been there.

"Decided to take him home," suggested Keele acidly.

It was too close. I gasped. "Home?"

But if Keele had guessed, Hinkley had missed it.

"He worked there," he snapped. "He was a sprayer."

Worked? I hadn't thought of any of them actually working. But they'd have to, come to think of it, when the necessity was to obtain access to the vehicles they needed. Then I registered that Hinkley knew all about Martin Astel, how the car had been used, and by whom. He was stringing me on. All he couldn't understand was why I'd gone there in the first place. I decided to make it more acceptable.

"It was Mr Keele who gave me the idea," I said.

Keele sat back. "Me?"

"When you told me all about the wedding cars being stolen. I linked that—"

Hinkley cut in. "You told him that, Sergeant?"

Keele looked uneasy. "It was part of the process of parting him from those wedding photos, sir. You'd think they were gold."

Hinkley eyed him for a moment. He reached out absently for his cigarettes and extracted a bent one. Then he returned to me.

"You were saying?"

I felt a bit better. I plunged on. "I linked what the sergeant had told me with what I'd worked out about the police car, and decided that'd been stolen as well. And I reckoned the best thing they could've done with it after- wards would've been to take it back to what I guessed was a repair place, and as I knew one . . ."

"You've said all this."

I bounded on, irrespective. "And as a fake copper had pinched my negatives, and as I guessed he was the same one on my wedding shot . . ."

"*What* same one?"

"A policeman," I stammered. I'd made a mistake. "Looked like one, anyway. To go with that car."

"There is no policeman in the set of prints you gave to Sergeant Keele."

The voice bounced from those tight walls and seemed to come at me from all sides, until the echoes lapsed to lingering silence.

"Not in *that* set," I mumbled.

"Then where?"

"In the set I printed for myself. It wasn't particularly a wedding shot, you see. So it's not in the other set. It's in the wallet that was stolen from the studio."

"All this bloody talk to get round to the only fact that matters. Let's hear about him."

"There's nothing to say. It must've been why he pinched 'em."

"I can see that."

"Which was why I wanted to find the car. He could've been using it—still—when he came to my place and broke in. They *could* have been in the car, at Casualty Thingy."

It was only marginally acceptable.

"But they weren't."

I thought it was a question. "I didn't look. It kind of put me off."

"They weren't. We've stripped the car."

76

I looked disappointed. "I was going to ask you for them."

"You'd be lucky."

"Yes. Reckon I would."

"When you don't move an inch towards helping us . . ."

"I've done what I could."

"You could have phoned us. You didn't have to cut out half a fence . . ."

Oh, he'd let me in! I'd wanted a distraction, preferably aimed at Keele's head.

"But I did," I said quickly. Hinkley was shredding his cigarette. "I phoned the one I thought was in charge of all this." Hinkley's colour mounted. "But he didn't seem interested. Mr Keele seemed more interested in telling me—"

"Sergeant?" Deadly, that was.

Keele stirred. "I thought he'd woken me at midnight to start bleating about his soddin' photographs . . ."

Hinkley's fist finally finished the pack. "That's exactly what he's been telling us for the past hour."

"He could've come out with it," said Keele with surly belligerence.

"He's not the sort who comes out with anything. You have to draw it out like a sore tooth."

I tried a weak sort of smile. "Better out than in."

"So now," said Hinkley, "I am here, at three-thirty, drawing it out, when you could've been on it at midnight."

"It's that woman of his," I confided to Hinkley, trying to find Keele a reason if not an excuse.

Hinkley looked at me. "Just get up out of that chair,"

he told me, "open that door, turn left, and keep going." He was painfully gentle.

I thought it best at that point to say no more. I did as he said. Left took me directly through an entrance lobby and out into fresh air.

At one time I had not expected to smell crisp June air again. With deep, appreciative breaths I savoured it. Cool, you understand, at nearly four in the morning. The sun would be up soon. Hell, I realised, it'd be blazing high before I got my car back. I was a good three miles from Darrow Engineering, and as far as I could tell there was no alternative to walking.

I began to walk. It did not occur to me to wait until later in the morning and take a bus. There was a lot of expensive equipment locked in that car. So I walked briskly, enjoying the experience, and realised that I was being followed.

This chap wasn't being subtle about it. Perhaps I was supposed to understand that I was under observation. For one moment I even wondered whether it could be Sergeant Keele, intent on catching me in a patch of deep shade, destined to become darker with my blood. But no, he'd still surely be engaged with his Inspector. All the same, it was an eerie feeling, just he and I alone in those deserted and threatening streets, alone apart from one solitary vehicle way behind . . .

It was accelerating. At the sound of its engine I stood and stared. It became a Landrover. The follower began to run, but he didn't have a chance. Comus Astel braked hard beside me and threw the passenger's door open. Somebody put two fingers in his mouth and gave a shrill whistle. We were moving before I had the door shut, and

I leaned out. A Cortina was drawing up beside the pedestrian.

"They're after us," I said.

"I know." Comus grinned briefly at me. "You balled it up, right enough. It's a good job I didn't trust you."

I hung on. He was taking corners like that. "Not trust me to what?"

"Take him back where he came from."

He had mentioned Petar Ješić's prowess with a car. If he'd been better than Comus, I was sorry I'd missed it. There was no traffic Comus could dodge in; no lights he could use, because reds are as good as greens at that time. But he held that Landrover on the edge of tyre adhesion and hurled it round corners even after, it seemed to me, he had passed them. The Cortina fell back.

"What did you expect me to do?" I asked.

"Run it straight to the police station."

"They didn't give me the chance."

"No?" He glanced at me. His eyes were set very deep, unreadable. "It was as good as." Then his voice became that fraction too casual. "How come they let you go?"

I told him how they'd come to let me go. He listened, one eye for his rear-vision mirror, the rocking car shooting off here and there in all directions. He had time to laugh in the right places.

"It wasn't funny."

"Depends how you tell it."

"Where're we going?"

"To pick up your car."

"Seems a long way round."

"I know this district, if you don't. Every street and

minor road. It's part of the background when we set up a job."

I turned and looked back. The Cortina was no longer there. "Then tell me," I asked, "why we have to do it in this hectic way. It's not illegal to collect your own car, so why're we trying to drop 'em? And," I suddenly thought, "how are we managing to drop them, when they'll know the district as well as you, and police drivers are experts?"

"They're not the police," he said, and he got us on two wheels turning into Darrow's car park.

I had left the Prefect tucked in a corner behind the cycle shed. The vast expanse of Darrow's park was deserted, the gates wide open. Comus spotted my car, and brought us to a dead-wheel stop beside it.

"Get moving fast," he shouted. "I'll try to block 'em."

I hadn't even got my keys in my hand. I fumbled, dropped them, a fear in me which must have come from the urgency in his voice. Then I found I'd left the door open, got in, put my key in the ignition lock, and a man's voice told me to hold it right there. Something hard rested behind my ear.

The rear door opened. I did not dare look round. The Cortina rocked into the park, tapping the gatepost with its tail, and the Landrover was not moving. The voice behind me said: "Out." I could tell by the voice that he'd have mean eyes and a thick neck. I got out, my legs weak. Comus was standing beside his Landrover with his hands well clear of his sides, facing a stocky man with hardly any legs, who was pointing a sawn-off shotgun at his stomach.

"We're not armed," he said.

My friend still behind me edged sideways away from the Prefect, so that I could see him. He had the mean eyes but not the neck. He was a streak, six feet three if an inch, mournful and hungry. I realised what Comus had meant by that big nothing. It gaped at me, and I was paralysed.

Out of the back door of the Cortina was coming a plump man, a florid man with a naked head and naked eyebrows. It was he who had the thick neck. Dainty hands and feet, though, a dainty manner, a delicate way with the pistol in his right hand, which he'd taken from his driver.

"Well," he said, walking round Comus. "Well, well. A bonus. If it isn't Comus Astel. In the flesh."

"Hello Quayle."

"Get your stuff," said Quayle casually. I realised he meant me, because the thin one prodded me with his gun.

"My stuff?"

"In the car. Lucky you got it with you." All this without a glance at me. "We'll take the Landrover, Minnit. Didn't reckon on bonuses."

"Sure chief," agreed the streak mournfully. "Get your stuff, crumb."

So I got my stuff, the two carry-alls with nearly £2,000 worth of equipment, and went to sit in the back of the Landrover with Comus, Minnit and the one with no legs whose name seemed to be Carraway, and we all went for a drive into the country, chasing the sun when it rose.

But I did not enjoy the ride. I'm ashamed to say that in spite of my fear I fell asleep inside the first ten miles.

# *Seven*

The halting car woke me. We were parked on the wide frontage to a low, extended bungalow. The sun was well up. Trees almost completely surrounded us. The tarmac was a deep red colour, as though blood had coursed along it. One door to the three-car garage was raised, and a big Merc lurked inside. Curtains at three of the windows were still closed.

We jumped down, Carraway and Minnit following us. Quayle had been driving the Cortina, and when he got out the driver of the Landrover switched over, sliding in behind the wheel of the Cortina. This was probably standard practice, the driver always ready for a smart getaway. I was surprised. I'd thought this was Quayle's place, which Comus had called Beatings. But there was a class to the place that was not Quayle's; there was an affluence that belonged, and had not been acquired viciously. Quayle would not mow a lawn so neatly, unless it was perhaps with a machine gun.

A man opened the door. He looked like nothing, a miserable apology of a man in his early twenties, all hair and teeth and ingratiation. All that made him something was a pistol in his right hand. His bangles shook and jingled.

'C . . . come on, chief. Where you bin?" He was vibrating with tension.

"Where's Bloomer?"

"Inside."

"I hope you kept it tight."

"Not a bleedin' m . . . murmur."

"You've been on the stuff again!"

And the youth cringed.

Comus caught my eye. I saw his head move in a fractional negation. No. Do nothing. Wait. There wasn't anything I could do, but I was in a better position for waiting. It seemed necessary for Comus to be urged from time to time with the hard end of Carraway's sawn-off.

We entered in procession, Quayle as though leading a delegation, me behind him, then the gawky Minnit, handling his gun languidly, then Comus, head up and eyes everywhere, his hands still away from his sides, and finally Carraway, taking two paces to our one.

A parquet hall with a side table loaded with flowers, above it a Monet print, a side door, open, through which I glimpsed a toilet seat, and ahead of us, also open, double glass doors opening into a wide and deep lounge.

A man leaned negligently against the mantel of an empty fireplace. He was around sixty, with grizzled grey hair and a goatee beard and big hands, big ears. Bloomer, they'd called him. A nervous tic ran down his left arm, jerking the pistol spasmodically. His casual air was a pose. He was tense, vibrant. He was watching a man and a woman, who were tied to two chairs.

They spread out, Quayle's men. I saw them then in a group, how they moved, how they stood, and recalled what Comus had said about Quayle's nerves. It had transmitted itself, like an owner to his dog. They were bouncing with it.

But who could blame them? The strain under which

83

they existed must have been enormous. And they had not only suffered the abrupt loss of two of their members, but had also endured the strain of the robbery, for nothing. I can imagine it'd be a traumatic experience to pull off an armed robbery—and just imagine the distress involved in discharging a shotgun in a bank cashier's face, or striking down any old ladies who might have the temerity to object. It seems to me that only the law ever exercises sufficient majesty of imagination to appreciate the cost in wear and tear to such thugs. I mean, time and again the courts clearly feel that the convicted have by then suffered more than enough, and admonish them with a fine or a stiff binding-over.

The woman's face had a weal down one cheek, the man had a bruise on his forehead and a flat nose. The blood had caked on his lips. In a distant room a child was screaming, screaming.

Comus was pale with strain.

I said: "What's all this?"

Quayle strutted. He used the floor like a stage, treading it delicately, indicating his mastery over it. His hand flicked to his breast pocket with the expertise of a fast draw, though I was certain he had too much self-regard to go armed. He produced one of my proofs.

"We are being entertained," he said, "by the Secretary of the local Photographic Society."

The print was shaking in his fingers. His eyes were never still. I grabbed his wrist and whipped the print from him. Four weapons centred on me, but I wasn't noticing particularly. That anger was on me again, burning slow but deep.

Oh, it'd be easy. You want the use of a studio and

darkroom, do you? Then look in the local directory, and there they are, all the clubs and societies in the area, with their officials. So you choose one and go round and politely ask for the use of the facilities, emphasising with occasional blows from a gun barrel.

"You," said Quayle, jerking a finger at me, "can do a copy of that. Blow it up, good and big. Something I wanta see."

About half a dozen thoughts clashed in my brain, making me dizzy. "*He* could've done that," I shouted. I pointed at the poor chap in the chair. "It didn't have to be me."

"You're the pro."

"Then you could've brought it to me, and I'd have done it at my place. Cost you a quid, perhaps . . ."

But Quayle's eyes stilled for a moment as he regarded me. They were cold, and completely without understanding. It had got into his blood. Nothing could be done without the futile gesture of violence. It was expected of him. He probably couldn't buy a first-class stamp without thumping a nose in emphasis. I was silent.

Comus said: "Do what he wants, Len."

I looked down at the print in my hand with despair. I already knew I couldn't do what Quayle wanted.

It was one of my wedding set, taken at the reception. Now I came to look at it, this was one of those taken during the toasts. It was the toast to the bridesmaids, given by the best man. There was Ljubica and her friend giggling away, and Comus's raised glass, only I'd been concentrating on the girls. What else? I'd caught Comus with the glass raised in his left hand, obscuring his face.

"Good and big," said Quayle threateningly.

"What on earth for?" My voice was dull.

"I wanta see his hand."

Now *that* left me cold. I looked at the hand and the glass. "I can see it."

"But can you see his little finger? Ahah! Can you?"

And for some reason the entire group burst into nasty laughter. I looked around. Comus had his lips drawn sideways in what could have been a bitter smile.

"I can see it."

"All of it?"

And they cackled obscenely.

I looked again. Two fingers and a thumb poised the glass. The third finger was bent. The little finger was crooked inwards. The shadow cut it off at the first joint.

"Not all of it," I confessed.

I was confused, not knowing what was meant by it, and then Comus slowly raised his left hand, his eyes steady and still that half-amused smile on his lips. The little finger on his left hand lacked the last two joints.

Then I knew what was meant, and I felt exhausted with the drain of it. I could do nothing, nothing.

When my eyes cleared I saw that this was not one of my copy prints. The colour and detail were too good for that. It was an original proof, one of the two sets I'd done at the beginning.

"Where did you get this?"

"Watch your mouth, sonny."

"I've got a reason."

"In there's all you'll need." He pointed to a door. How the devil could he know what I needed? "Get with it," said Quayle.

I took a breath. "You're asking me . . ."

86

He casually turned, and lashed out with the back of his hand. Just where Comus had caught me. For a minute I was blinded. I shook my head and tried again.

"It's impossible to copy this and bring out . . ." I took a step back on to Minnit's gun. ". . . more than you can already see."

Quayle sneered. "I seen it done. On the films and on the tele."

"That's a fake. It can't be done."

"You . . ." He stuck a finger almost up my nose. ". . . do it."

I was encouraged by a prod from Minnit's gun. I took a deep breath. "Then produce the negative. I might be able to do it from that."

"What's he on about?" asked Minnit drearily. "He makes me tired."

The grizzled old veteran growled in his throat. "Let's get on with it." He wasn't wearing his teeth. He spat on the carpet.

"We ain't got no negative," said Quayle. "We got *that*. Now get moving."

I turned it over, feeling despair. On it was printed: ASK HIM WHERE HE WAS AFTER THE BANK JOB

Then I knew. I looked up, and saw that Comus had already realised.

"But he was there! There at the reception. I saw him. We all saw him . . ." My voice failed with my heart.

I could not remember seeing him, but that was no doubt because he'd been out with the Chief Superintendent's car radio. They wouldn't take my word for it, anyway. They had been tipped off that Comus had been in that police car, as planned, had hunted their getaway car to a crash, had killed their men, and had got away with what they'd obviously consider to be their money. And killed Petar Ješić? I choked on that thought.

"I cannot do . . ."

"Get on—"

". . . what you're asking," I shouted, ignoring the prods, the big nothings centred on me. "Ask *him*. He'll know."

But the man in the chair stared at me with terrified, pleading eyes, and said nothing. He'd know, well enough. But he wasn't about to commit himself.

"Do it," said Comus gently.

When all that could save him would be an enlargement clearly showing a missing finger! How the hell could I show something not there? *That* was the big nothing.

I said: "Let's see what we've got to work with." Stalling, terrified, and reaching for time.

The owner had divided a large room into two smaller ones, a darkroom and a studio. There was a spot and a couple of floods in the studio, and apparently he used the plain wall as a background. All right for portraits, but I couldn't see much that'd help me. In the darkroom he was more fully equipped. There was a long counter with cupboards beneath and a double stainless steel sink. He had a decent colour enlarger, a Durst, and a wall cupboard was well supplied with paper. His chemicals were in the cupboard beneath the sink, two developing tanks, one 35mm and one 120 size. So far so good, if I'd been seriously intending to photograph my own proof, develop the negative, then blow up a print to twelve by sixteen, say.

But I had not been fooling. You cannot copy a print and bring out more than there is already. Maybe if I could have glazed it, we might have brought out some slight gradation of light and shade or of colour around the palm shadow in which the little finger was hidden. But I'd printed on a silk surface, and my host didn't have a glazing machine anyway. And what could it prove? Only, at the worst, that there was a whole finger on that left hand, and that therefore Comus Astel had not been there to propose the toast to the bridesmaids.

Which, in the prevailing circumstances, was not what I had any great desire to achieve.

There was no way of using the enlarger stand as a copier.

"Sellotape," I said, impatiently, snapping my fingers. Carraway began to search frantically in the drawers. At any other time I'd have been amused.

We were in the darkroom at that time, Comus and myself, being watched by Carraway and Minnit. Outside in the lounge the other three were relaxing, with only the bound couple to control.

"This it?" Carraway had found a roll of masking tape.

Minnit stirred impatiently. "Let him find his own stuff."

Carraway retrieved his sawn-off from the bench, looking sheepish. This was a character who'd have fawning respect for anybody with any ability at all, because he possessed only one. I glanced at Comus, who was lounging against the wall. His eyelid flickered fractionally.

I made a reasonable-looking job of it, taping the print to the wall in the studio, fixing my Canon, with the f/3.5 macro lens, to our friend's very practical studio tripod, and using the two floods. In practice, I'd have got a decent result. I had a couple of frames left on the spool. I used them. I unscrewed the camera, detached the print, and we trooped out into the lounge again, and back towards the darkroom.

"How much longer?" demanded Quayle. He was pacing nervously.

"A couple of hours."

"Not on your bloody life. I'll give you twenty minutes."

The phone rang on a side table. We all looked at it and nobody moved. His office ringing to enquire where he was?

"Fifteen!" he shouted angrily.

"What d'you think this is?" I demanded. "A Polaroid?"

Quayle gave a howl and dived for the pistol being held limply by the hairy youth. The blood drained from my face.

"Shoot me and it'll be longer," I told him. "You're wasting time."

He made a disgusted sound. We retired into the darkroom. Comus lounged in his corner again, with Minnit leaning back on the door. Carraway was beside me at the bench. He watched me wind the film back into the cassette, open the back of the camera, and extract it. He was frowning with intense concentration. I thought I had a recruit.

"That's the shutter, look." I pointed. "The film comes across here, over this sprocket . . ."

While I was talking I'd arrayed on the bench what I'd need, the tank, lid off, and the spool to one side, two twenty-ounce beakers and a larger one, the thermometer—the air temperature was 20°C, close enough. I began to reach out bottles of prepared chemicals. They were proper chemist's bottles with glass stoppers. Obligingly, Carraway reached over to help me.

"Don't *touch* that one!" I cried, as he opened his pudgy paw.

He drew back as though stung. I was putting on rubber gloves. I always use gloves, because some of the chemicals can affect your skin.

"That's pure acid, mate," I said. "Let me do it."

I placed the bottle carefully and gently on the bench, out of harm's way. Then I looked at how things were sighted. You'll remember what comes next, of course. You're right. I reached over and put out the light.

There was a scuffle, an oath. Something clattered to the floor. Then the light came on again.

Minnit was standing with his finger on the switch, his weapon darting about, his eyes like brittle, dancing beads. I stood with my spool of film in my left hand, Comus was still relaxed in his corner, and Carraway was recovering his shotgun from the floor.

The breath hissed through Minnit's teeth. ". . . the hell!"

I told him: "It's got to be completely dark. *Got* to be."

"Oh no you don't. Think we're stupid?"

I sighed. "Then tell Quayle it's off."

The eyes darted. The mind stumbled blindly behind them. "We gotta talk."

So, out we trooped again.

"Now what?" Quayle was close to dancing.

"This character says he's got to be in the dark."

91

"What you pulling?" Quayle demanded, advancing on me.

The hairy one had his gun back. He leered, showing brown teeth, and prodded the gun in my general direction. I reckoned he might hit the wall.

"Ask him," I said, nodding to the man in the chair.

It was a mistake. Quayle couldn't just ask. He lashed the man across the face with the back of his hand. "Is that true?"

His mouth was almost sealed with dried blood. He had difficulty prising his lips apart. "Yes," he whispered.

I was learning, though. No more appeals. I was on my own.

"Then get inside with him," Quayle snarled at Minnit. "Put a gun in his back . . ."

"Not me," said Minnit. "With him in the dark . . ."

He'd be six inches taller than me, had a gun in his hand, and he was scared!

"Then I'll do it on my own."

"Minnit!"

I knew then why Quayle was running this lot. He had the edge of vicious destructiveness. Minnit said: "Ah . . ." Then he took it out on me with a kick aimed at my ankle, which caught my heel harmlessly because I was already on my way back into the darkroom.

I got the film into the spiral, there in the dark, my hands unsteady because the gun barrel was borning holes in my kidneys, and Minnit's breath was hot and rank on the back of my neck. I locked on the lid.

"You can put the light on now."

He did so.

92

"You see," I told him. "Quite painless, and it's in the tank."

His awareness that I'd recognised his fear took him to the brink of murder. I saw it in his eyes. We stood like that a moment, one indrawn breath apart, then Quayle's voice broke it up.

"What's with you in there, damn you?"

"Ready," I called.

It seemed that something about my attitude, some confidence perhaps, which was no more than my natural concentration on what was after all my main interest in life, had conveyed itself to Minnit. He was on edge, expecting something from me. He was nervous of being alone with me. Flattering, I found that.

He called in Carraway to back him up. This, apparently, disturbed Quayle, who realised that it left Comus under the restraint of only two guns, one held by a hop-head. There was a respect for Comus, who was now so relaxed that I wondered how he managed not to collapse. As his languor grew, so did Quayle's tension—perhaps he knew something. So Quayle sent Comus back into the darkroom with us, and we resumed our positions, Carraway and me at the bench, Minnit leaning against the door, Comus in his corner.

I began to pour the chemicals into the flasks. I plopped the thermometer into the colour developer flask and set the timer. Then I carefully lifted the bottle I'd described as acid and poured it, concentrating, into another flask. Carraway watched with fascination. I picked up the flask and poised it above the tank, though I had no intention of ruining a film with a first bath of bleach.

Then I threw it in Carraway's face.

He screamed. It would do no more than render him a little paler, perhaps, but to Carraway his eyes were burning out and his skin smoking. I caught the sawn-off on its way down, turned, and fired at Minnit's gun hand. But with all my tensed speed, I was too slow. Already Minnit was collapsing sideways with a dislocated jaw, and Comus had his gun. The narrow stream of shot tore a hole through the door, mid-way between their heads.

"Pump it," shouted Comus. He fired two shots through the hole, and I heard a scream outside. I was pumping it, a smoking shell flying out over my shoulder. Comus took the door and frame out with his foot, there being no time to draw it open towards us. Then we ran out into the lounge.

The youth had a dead arm swinging loose with blood dripping from it. He was keening in a high, pitiful voice. His gun lay on the floor. Quayle saw us coming and dived for the gun, and I blasted a hole in the carpet a foot in front of his hand. The veteran fired, casually, the shot whipping my shoulder, then Comus shot the gun out of his hand.

"Your back!" shouted Comus, thinking quicker than I was.

I turned. Minnit was supporting himself against the door jamb, laughing twistedly, no fear in him now that the tension had gone. I put the shotgun under his nose, and he spat his contempt sideways down the barrel. I pumped it again, and the contempt disappeared with the spent shell.

Quayle was running for the door, dragging the youth by one arm, Bloomer by the other. I saw that Comus was letting them go.

"Get your friend," I said.

Minnit turned back. Carraway was a wet, sobbing heap on the darkroom floor.

"He'll be all right. May turn grey, though."

Minnit dragged him out. The car outside revved into life, and Minnit moved faster. We reached the front door as it pulled round and accelerated away, one door still open, one short, inadequate leg dangling from it.

# Eight

Comus was running towards the Landrover with loping strides. I could see that he might be averse to scattering corpses all over someone's carpet, but was quite capable of leaving a car-load of them somewhere in a ditch.

"Wait!" I shouted.

I was not prepared to leave my equipment in a stranger's house, nor to return for it at a time when the police might be in attendance. Comus stopped. In any event, firearms were banging away from the windows of the Cortina now, and it was still odds of five to two.

Five to one and a half, really; my abrupt burst of destructive enthusiasm had left me, and I was limp and shaking with the reaction. But Comus seemed happy enough to wait by the Landrover.

I got my stuff together. There was no possibility of taking my film out of the tank, so I took that too. I paused in the lounge and fetched out my penknife. I was still thinking like a gunman, not prepared to have anybody reach a phone until we were halfway down their drive.

I cut the woman free. I bent and kissed her on the forehead as I did so. "Sorry, love." Then I left the sawn-off on the mantelpiece as a souvenir, and ran for the Landrover.

I asked Comus to drive carefully. "Give my nerves a break, there's a good chap."

"Where's the shotgun?"

"I left it."

"Fingerprints . . ."

"I'm still wearing the gloves."

"Huh!" He glanced at me. "I reckon they wouldn't be on file anyway."

It was kind of a question. "Of course not."

He was grave. "Just thinking—the way you handled that gun—you could have learned the ropes in a bank."

"And you! Kidding me you've never even loaded a gun."

"It's true. I've practised at a range. Targets. Somebody else loaded it."

I was silent. Then he sounded annoyed. "The ability's got to be there, in case you need it."

"So I gather. Oh, it was there right enough."

We drove on steadily. He was taking a tortuous route, so as to avoid the incoming flood of police cars. We were silent for a few minutes.

"D'you know where we are?" I asked at last.

"Not yet. We'll see a signpost some time."

"Don't forget, I've still got to pick up my car."

"I'd remembered."

A few more minutes. We hit a main road, and he knew where we were.

"I'm getting hungry," I said.

"You're like an old woman."

"It's all right for you . . . you're used to it."

"I am *not* used to it."

"What would they have done if you really hadn't been used to it, and you hadn't been able to get Minnit fast enough and wing the hairy one, and shoot that gun out of Bloomer's hand, and . . ."

He swerved into the forecourt of a roadside café, and we went in for bacon, egg and chips and three cups of coffee.

"In around five minutes," he said, "Quayle would've cut his losses and assumed it wasn't me toasting the bridesmaids." He sipped his third coffee. "Then he'd have taken me away somewhere—to Beatings prob-bably—and used all his ingenuity to persuade me to tell him where I'd hidden the money."

"Which you wouldn't have been able to do?"

"Because I don't know where it is."

"Of course not," I said politely.

"He's got to you!"

"Made me think."

"I warned you about that."

"I reckon I've got a right to the odd thought or two, in between the bits of action."

He grinned, and tapped me on the knuckle with a spoon. "All right. One thought you're allowed. Which is?"

"What would Quayle have done with *me*?"

He shrugged. "Shot you through the stomach and left you on the carpet."

"Hmm!" I looked him in the eye. "And those people?"

"He'd have been mad by then. It's like a shot of Vitamin B to him. He'd have killed them too."

I felt a little less sick about what we'd done to their home.

Comus's eyes were steady. There was a strong line round his jaw, and I'd have trusted him with my Access card. We'd been tossing it around, not feeling the texture of it, not admitting that Quayle was real. But there was a hard knot of fear and disgust in my stomach, and there was nobody to hold my hand. Access card perhaps, but my hand? I wasn't sure.

I looked away from him. "Let's get moving."

We headed home. I let the silence build up. It was almost as though Comus waited for me, or as though he didn't trust himself to intrude on the thoughts he'd permitted me.

At last: "Somebody doesn't like you," I said.

"Quite a number I suppose. I don't make an effort to be liked. It doesn't get you anywhere in this world. And I'm impatient. I give orders and expect people to jump. I slap people around. I snarl at them. No, I'm not liked."

He didn't have to sound so proud of it, did he? "That wasn't what I meant, and you know it. Perhaps you're just a convenience."

"People have tried to treat me like that."

"This print . . ." I had it in my pocket, and produced it. "Did you see . . . but of course you didn't. It says on the back—obviously a message to Quayle—for him to ask you where you got to after the robbery happened."

"I guessed it was something like that."

"Don't you see what that means?"

"As you said—I'm not liked," he said.

"Try to be serious," I snapped. "This is you we're talking about. This is one of the original proofs, which were pinched. They were taken by a copper—somebody pretending to be a copper . . . one of *your* lot . . ." I paused. He did not react. "Did you, or did you not," I shouted, "have a police car there with Ruźa's brother at the wheel and another chap waiting to jump in beside him when your getaway car got going . . ."

"It wasn't quite like that."

99

"How was it then?"

"Calm down. I'll tell you. We didn't have a getaway car. The basic idea was confusion. Six of us would've done the bank job, then the police car would've blurred the issue, the money would've found its way into the bride's car . . ."

"The white Jag, which just happened to be the Chief Super's? I suppose that was pure chance?"

"A nice touch, I thought," he admitted placidly. "Anyway, the six of us would fade into the background of the wedding, the police car would blind off after an imaginary escape car, and its radio would draw the real police in the opposite direction."

"Right. That's fine. I've got a clear picture. So *your* fake policeman got his smirking mug on one of my shots. And when he came to think about it, he didn't like the idea. You see, there'd been a cashier killed, and that wasn't what he'd bargained for, and there was every chance the police'd be round to see what interesting facts I might have recorded on film."

"As they did."

"A bit too late. But of course, there was the second set of proofs in existence. Maybe I worked a bit too fast for him. Very unprofessional. But it was easy enough to get hold of the only two prints that interested him, because the set was circulating like a tornado amongst all the little Jeśićs and their friends . . ." I paused. Comus didn't comment. I went on. "Do you doubt it was *your* policeman, now? Who else could've got his hands on the negatives *and* the two prints from Ruźa's set?"

He was negotiating an island. I knew where we were now. He could throw me out any time, and I'd still

100

manage to get home.

He spoke consideringly. "It could have been two separate people."

"Don't kid me. But he was lucky, as it happens."

"How's that?"

"My memory. I can usually recall any of my pictures. But not this one—not *his* face. I'll get it though. Given time. But in the meantime he's beautifully anonymous. To me, that is. To Quayle and to the police, too. But you must know him, this friend who sent the picture to Quayle."

"I know him."

"So that now, as soon as you've dropped me, you'll be heading straight to the Ješićs' . . ."

"He doesn't live there."

"Heading for where he lives, then—and you've still got Minnit's gun in your pocket."

"You'd noticed?"

"Yes. So I'm not going to let you drop me as easy as that. I'll be on your tail, Comus. I'm not having you shooting him full of holes . . ."

"Why'd I do that?"

"Because he framed you, you fool."

"I didn't realise that."

"Will you stop talking like that!"

"Like what?"

"All casual. I know you now. The more casual you get, the more dangerous you are."

He laughed. He reached in his pocket and produced the gun. It was a large automatic.

"Here, you have it then."

"I don't want it!"

101

"Keep me safe from myself."

"Somebody's got to look after you."

"Well now, I've got a protector!"

"You tried to stop me from thinking. It doesn't mean you've got to stop, too. Doesn't it worry you that you've been framed?"

"I care."

I could have killed him. Hell, I had the gun in my hand. "I could kill you. Doesn't it occur to you that now those two other photos are missing, there's absolutely nothing to show you were even at the reception. Listen, you big idiot, the negatives don't matter . . ."

"Oh, first I've heard of that. When you've been bleating on about 'em . . ."

"Don't matter in the reasoning," I said tightly. "The important thing isn't what was on those two. It could be what isn't on any of the others. That's what matters. I see it now, I've been slow."

"And what was not on the others?" he asked.

"You, Comus, you."

We had reached the Darrow Engineering car park. Somehow, I'd expected it to be the same, but it was mid-morning, fork-lift trucks were in the making, and the park was packed with vehicles. My Prefect was tucked neatly behind the cycle shed—which had no cycles in it—and boxed-in by the Rover 3500s and Jaguar 4.2s.

I got out of the Landrover and considered the situation. A works policeman approached.

"This your car, sir?"

"Yes. I'm sorry. Had some trouble with it last night, and I thought it was best to get it off the road."

You can see how glibly I was lying by that time. It's the practice that does it.

He was a little, military-looking man, very pleasant. "We could see you've had trouble. The door's broken open, and it's had a bash up the back." And he marched briskly to his hut.

Of course, Minnit and Carraway had broken open the door to get in. I couldn't see why they'd dent the back of my boot in, though, as they clearly hadn't been searching for my equipment. It had been on the back seat. But bashed it was, and the lid wouldn't open. That put me in a right spot, because now I'd have nowhere to lock away my stuff if I wanted to leave it in the car.

We waited. The factory's Tannoy began to request the owners of the following cars to report to the main gate, and a list of numbers was recited. I felt embarrassed. Comus stood and watched me becoming warm. He could have dropped me, after all, as easy as snap your fingers. But he waited. I then realised what for. I hadn't finished what I'd been saying.

"It was you who wasn't on the rest, Comus. My memory! I got a shot of you arriving with your brother, and you were probably on that first group with the grinning copper. But after that . . . no. Somebody said you were shy . . ."

"I am."

"I've known all-in wrestlers who're shy of a camera."

"*You have?*"

"What's so strange about that? I was a sports photographer for a national daily. But you . . ."

"You're going to say I wasn't there to be taken?"

"I don't remember your face on any more."

103

"Except the toast one."

"Your face!"

"But you must have *seen* me . . . around."

"I don't remember that."

"With that wonderful memory!" he said derisively.

"Even with that."

"But . . . the toast."

"That," I said, "could have been a stand-in."

"But everybody would've seen it was me."

"And would they have said?"

"Of course . . ." He stopped. "Oh Lord!"

They began to arrive. I had, it seemed, chosen the executive corner of their car park. Managing Director, Managers, Secretaries and Treasurers, they all trooped out to rescue me. They were very pleasant about it. I suggested that a simpler solution would be to find me a position on the staff, but there were no takers. I suddenly yearned for a safer job than photography.

At last I was free. We got it out into the road. They waved as I drove away, the Landrover following. I pulled in and parked, got out and walked back, and climbed in beside Comus.

"Cut your engine," I said. "We hadn't finished. You're probably unique, mate. The only person with a dead-solid alibi—at a reception with a hundred people . . ."

"Eighty-one."

"And everybody willing to say you were there. But not one bit of it any good. Because you'd probably *need* an alibi. All six or so of you would, in case anything went wrong at the bank and you had to head for wide-open spaces. So . . . it'd be laid on. Eighty-one people would swear you were there when you weren't. And they'd be disbelieved by the police. The same eighty-one would also swear you were there when you *were*. And they'd be disbelieved. Hell, you've got an alibi, and it's worth nothing.''

"Got me nicely caught, ain't you!''

"And there's only one thing that'll prove you were there at the reception, and that's my one shot with you on it, holding a glass in front of your face and not showing the end of your pinkie.''

He drew his palms down his face. He stopped doing it, and peered at me above seven and a half of his fingers. "And you think I'll need to prove that?''

"To me you do, anyway.''

"That was what I thought.''

"And there's only one way of doing it. The negatives. With *them*, I can knock up enlargements, and really have a chance with gradations and colours, and maybe . . . just maybe . . . I can get a blow-up that'll *show* that the fingers holding that glass have got two joints missing off your pinkie.''

"You crafty bastard!'' he burst out. "The way you've worked round to that! All you ever wanted was to get your hands on those negatives.''

"It's what I've always said.''

"So now I've got to help you do it.''

"I don't see why you're so reluctant,'' I burst out. "The rotten swine tried to frame you.''

"Only for Quayle's benefit,'' he said softly. "Quayle's stupid, so logic wouldn't help. For everybody else . . . it'd be obvious it wasn't me in the car.''

"I don't see that.''

"Petar Ješić was shot. I'd never do that. He was my friend. Petar taught me to drive. You should've seen him, dropping down from ninety to take a sharp bend, using all the gears, double de-clutching so fast you couldn't follow it, and pulling away . . ."

"All right. I believe you. Perhaps everybody but Quayle would, too."

"No," he said, poking me in the ribs. "You *don't* believe me. It'd be you I was proving it to."

"And you'd have a nice big picture to show the Judge."

He laughed, and punched me on the shoulder. "Then we'll do it tonight. You'll get your negatives."

I didn't like that. "Now."

"You need some sleep. And he works nights."

"I suppose he would."

"So get off home, and I'll ring you."

"Don't ring me—I'll ring you." I'd heard that one before. I was half way to the ground. I paused. "Do you think I ought to go back there?"

He leaned over. "Why not?"

"Quayle knows where I am. He might send Carraway . . ."

"Then take the gun. You can look after yourself. I've seen."

"Not in cold blood I can't. And there's Sergeant Keele. He'll want a word with me. Several."

"You certainly can't come round to the Ješićs'."

I found a wistful voice. "I'd like to see Ruža . . . apologise . . ."

"Get back in here!"

I got back in. He seized my arm. His teeth were inches

from my nose. "You can't stay there, you fool."

"Not till it's dark?"

"You're crazy."

"I'm scared."

He sighed. "I don't suppose you've got two beds?"

"I'll sleep on the chair. I really ought to get back, anyway. There's the cat."

"I'm a bloody nursemaid now. All right. You lead the way."

"You'll have to park this somewhere. There's only room for one round the back."

He thrust me out of the Landrover. His anger could have been quite genuine. He knew what I wanted, knew that I'd realised he wasn't wildly angry about the policeman having sent that print to Quayle, and that I guessed he might well warn him we were on our way. He knew I didn't trust him, and if there was going to be any proof involved I'd have to keep him in clear view for a few hours.

So we parked the Landrover behind the Town Hall in the Borough Engineer's slot, and went on to my place. The cat eyed me with disapproval, but cheered up when I produced his tin. I fed Comus and myself on chips and egg and frozen peas, and we slept until eight, he insisting on the chair. At least, *he* slept till eight. The buzzer went at three and I ran off a set of sixteen shots of a pleasant lady's peke. Then I returned and slept till eight.

We ate again. I played him Prokofiev on my tape deck, and he said he preferred Scott Joplin. So I played him Scott Joplin. We sat and we chatted and the cat stretched on his knees, and we never mentioned crime. We watched the sun go down over my roofs. He told me Ješić had a place in Wales and was thinking of retreating to it, strategically. After he'd settled with Quayle, that was.

Did I say we didn't speak of crime? But murder isn't really a crime, is it? Not the personal ones, I mean. They're not crimes against society, only against the individual. They ought to make it a civil offence. A debt. This defendant is sued in fee simple . . . in that he did take away the life of the plaintiff . . . who is not in court . . . and has failed to return it . .

I was dozing. Comus was putting on his jacket. He had the gun in his belt. "It's dark," he said. It was nearly midnight. I was beginning to live out of phase.

"Must we?" I groaned.

"Your idea."

So we did. I put out the lights and we felt our way down the back staircase. No point in advertising our clandestine movements. I eased the car out of its gap, the engine now behaving itself, and sedately we drove out of town.

To the west you hit country in a couple of miles. He hadn't told me, but I was getting wary by that time, so I kept an eye on the rear-view mirror. I saw nothing following us. Comus directed. I did as he said, and started to worry about the petrol gauge. I'm a chronic worrier.

"Not much further," he said.

There was a river. I could hear it but not see it. We crossed a bridge and turned sharply left, though the main road had a natural right bend just there. Now I saw the river beyond his shoulder, the moon catching chuckles in the fast water. Along our right was a rise of grassland. Higher, beyond it and dark against the sky, there was a row of select homes, placed for the view across the river and the valley.

"Slower," he murmured. I slowed "A turn on the right. Yes . . . there, look."

It was narrow and steep. I took the Prefect up in second. At the top a minor road, probably private, paralleled the river. We turned right again. He said:

"Park here. Under this tree."

I did. I cut the engine. Faintly the river trickled below. Somewhere an owl called. The houses were silent and dark.

We walked softly along the roadway. Steep drives sloped down to garages, which seemed to use the upper floors. "The bungalow," he whispered. I saw it. The grounds were larger than most; the building itself was smaller. It crouched and waited for us.

"You're sure he works nights?"

"He's a works policeman."

We circled it. We were on a terrace that seemed to be perched above space. There was no let-up from the moon, like a searchlight revealing us to the world. He put his lips to my ear.

"Stay here. I'll have a scout around. Don't move."

And then he left me. The moon seemed to ignore him and concentrate on me. One second he was a shadow. Then the shadow deepened and he fell into it.

There was an opening window directly in front of me, reaching to the ground. I crouched and stared into it, trying to see beyond the glass, but seeing only the reflection of that burning moon. I didn't even see movement behind me, no shadow, no uplifted arm.

Yet suddenly there was a blurred crescendo crash in my head, such as Bartok does with cymbals, and I was unconscious.

# Nine

The moon had disappeared. I seemed to be lying in the river, the chill all down my spine and the rill of the water louder, more persistent. Only pain stapled my head to my body. I moved my head gently. The pain did not tear free. My head was poised above the chill, and I was facing the room. The shape of it bloomed, then cleared, focussed, and I saw that the moon had left with the window, which now was wide open above and behind me. The water splashed on. The river flowed inside the house. A tap was running.

Suddenly I was hot and the thrilling water beckoned. On hands and knees I moved towards it and over the step. I stumbled to my feet, and fell. A chair rocked. A cabinet steadied me. I walked my hands up it and rested. The water ran on. The pain was easing. My sight was clearing, but it was dark. At my feet the moon shafted a spear of light. It seemed not to have moved.

I slid my feet, with growing confidence, towards the water. The door into the hall was open. With my hand on the wall I followed the sound to the right.

The venetian blinds in the kitchen were closed. The light was on. Comus stood at the kitchen sink, his head under the swivel outlet. He turned at the small sound I made, instantly crouched, his fists prepared. Then he relaxed.

"You too? Come on, let's have a look."

I allowed him to examine my head. He caught me by the neck and thrust my head beneath the water without warning. I choked.

"Skin's not broken. You'll do fine."

We stood, facing each other, water dripping from our lank hair. He laughed. "A right clever pair we are."

"He was here all the time?"

He shook his head—more than I could have managed. "Would he have gone away and left us here?"

A thought jolted me. "Then somebody's beaten us to it!" It was a cry of despair, like a lost child. I was very low, realising only then how the blow on the head had stricken me.

Comus put a hand on my shoulder, and I shook him off angrily.

"It's unlikely," he said reasonably. "Your photographs and stuff'll be in his wall safe, Len. Who's going to be able to get that open?"

"If you knew that, why the hell're we here?"

"Don't shout. And here, we'd better have the light off."

He crossed and put off the light. My last impression of his face was of calm confidence.

"I can get the safe open," he said. "I've had some practice."

What the devil was I doing here with a bank robber who could shoot pips out of playing cards and open safes? I had to force my mind to work that one out. I wanted my negatives, and Comus was the only one who could deliver them, that was why.

"You and your practice!" I said disgustedly. "I suppose you've got gelignite and heat lances . . . and . . .

and things."

"I've got this," he said, dangling something like an octopus in front of my blind eyes.

"Take it away. What is it?"

"A stethoscope."

I had never believed it. Oh, it looks good on the screen, but I couldn't accept that it was practical. It stands to reason that if it was possible to hear the tumblers, or whatever they use, then the manufacturers would have built-in a bit of soundproofing.

"I hope you can see to use it," I said sarcastically.

"It only needs educated ears."

"Sure you don't want the light on?"

"A chink of light in this room and you'd see it clear across the valley. Just be quiet a minute, while I find where he's hidden it."

He was trying the pictures by touch. The moonlight barely revealed that there was only one picture, over the fireplace. Who'd be stupid enough to hide his safe behind his only picture? Not this chappie, anyway. There was a blank wall behind it. There was a blank wall behind the tall mirror beside the french window.

"Perhaps he's got hinged wallpaper," I suggested.

"Be quiet!"

"Perhaps it's in another room."

It was behind a set of Encyclopaedia Britannica on a long shelf beside the fireplace.

"Neat," he said, turfing them out on to the carpet.

I watched with fascination. He was actually doing it, the stethoscope in his ears, the sensor on the metal beside the dial. His face was pale and concentrated in the moonlight.

"Don't tell me you can hear . . ."

"Want a listen?"

"No thank you."

He nodded, and went on with it, trying the door from time to time. Suddenly it swung open.

He handed them out. "Which is yours?" There was a long envelope containing what looked like a deed, a wad of bank notes in a rubber band, a thick something from Inland Revenue, and mine . . . my own wallet. I could hardly believe it.

"That yours?"

I nodded. It felt thick as though it was all there.

"Then let's put the rest back," he said.

"You're leaving him the money?"

You can be sarcastic once too often. He made a sharp, angry sound, and his hand clasped my wrist. "You've got what you came for," he said savagely.

"Sorry. Here."

He put them back and spun the cylinder. He slammed back the volumes of the encyclopaedia with unnecessary force.

"Let's get out of here." His voice was flat. I was definitely out of favour.

I headed for the open window. He said: "Careful."

"Of what?" It was me being curt now.

"Somebody knocked us out. They could still be around."

"They?" I'd assumed one person. I don't know why.

He put his head close to mine. "It'd have to have been almost simultaneous. Either one of us could've heard the other fall."

"I was crouching down."

113

"Don't quibble. I'd have heard the blow."

Good ears, Comus had. Good eyes, too, it seemed. He made me stay back, then he advanced to the far edge of the terrace, which had a low retaining wall. He got down on his stomach for the last few yards, only his eyes and his bedraggled hair—blurring his outline—above the edge. For two minutes he was very still. Then he waved for me to join him. I did exactly what he had done. The slope was steep beyond the terrace, the river standing out silver-sharp below, and just this side of it the dark grey stream of the road.

"There's a car down there," he breathed.

I couldn't see anything. "Where?"

"Watch."

He wriggled back. The moon was high. He swung the window shut. From below they would catch the moon's reflection as a flash. He was beside me again.

I saw movement down there. Where I had seen nothing, the changed shadows now resolved it. Cats work like that, alert to movement. A man had got out of a car and was standing beside it, his face a lighter disc turned upwards.

"Waiting for us," said Comus.

Perhaps waiting for Comus to empty the safe, perhaps waiting to get his hands on my negatives! I clutched them fiercely.

"Let's get out . . ."

"There's no way, except past that car."

"Then what do we do?"

We retreated from there, that's what we did. We went and sat in my car, and thought about it.

"I could go down and deal with them," he suggested.

114

I was very aware of the gun in his belt. "I don't want that."

"It depends who it is."

"Does it? I've had enough of guns."

"It could be Quayle. You wouldn't object to him?"

"If it was Quayle . . . hell, Comus, you know him. He wouldn't wait there, quietly. He'd be up here with everything going, and blast holes all over the place."

"Then it's the police."

"No guns, then." I was too deep in it already, involved in a shoot-out, and now a burglary. You didn't top it off with a copper or two lying in the roadway.

Comus seemed to read my thoughts. "We've got to keep you out of it, if it's the police. Otherwise you'll never be able to go back to your studio."

"I could already be in trouble, if it was them knocked us out."

"Does that sound like normal police procedure to you?"

"I'm not sure that Keele's normal."

I was beginning to realise the handicaps the police worked under. They had to operate by a set of rules, for the protection of the public. I reckon they mainly protected public enemies. I wasn't sure that Keele carried a rule book in his pocket; I was certain that his memory let him down from time to time when it came to operating them.

"I'll have to draw them off," said Comus.

"How?"

"Another car. We can't let 'em see this."

I nodded towards the bungalow. "His?"

"As he's clearly not here, he'll have his car with him.

No—next door's."

Next door there was a semi-bungalow, built into the slope. It had a two-car garage. "You'll pinch their car?"

"Borrow it. He won't mind."

"He won't get the chance."

He grinned, and got out. I picked his stethoscope from the seat. "Won't you need this?"

"I didn't need it before."

"Heh! Don't walk away. What's *that* mean?"

"It made it look good, for your benefit. Now don't get your blasted hackles up. It didn't have to seem too easy. I've got my pride."

"And I haven't? What the hell d'you mean?"

"They all leave something so's they don't have to remember the combination. I've even seen it written on a wall. Honest. The encyclopaedias, Len. Numbers two, five, nine and eleven were sticking out from the others. All I had to do was try the various series of those four numbers. Now let me get on with the next bit. It's harder."

I followed him. I made it twenty-eight permutations. He was working on the up-and-over door.

Here, we were on the shaded side of the building. I could barely see what he was doing. He seemed to have a large bunch of keys, and by touch found one that slid into the Yale-type lock of the door. That left his chances about a hundred thousand to one against having the correct profile. I waited for his failure. He simply moved the key in and out rapidly, putting gentle pressure on the door handle. It opened cleanly.

"You get all the pins bouncing," he whispered, as though I'd need to treasure the knowledge for the future.

116

There was one car in the garage, an Alfasud. The owner hadn't troubled to lock it. Hadn't he got a perfectly good lock on his door? I was gratified to see, though, that even Comus had no professional substitute for my length of wire. He found something which would do, and connected it up, twisting it tighter with his fingers than I could have done with pliers.

"Now we've got to push it out."

"Up that slope?"

He hissed at me angrily, impatient with my stupidity. "If we start it now, they'll be warned down there. Put your back into it, and don't argue."

Well enough for him to talk. The slope of the drive looked like the Matterhorn. We had to rock it even to get it moving, and then, of course, we could not afford to stop. My back creaked. Blood pounded in my head and my bump throbbed. We were side by side at the bonnet, Comus like a tractor. The car groaned up the drive, little pebbles cracking under the tyres.

We got it on the level. I sat down on the tarmac, panting.

"Now," said Comus, one arm through the window at the wheel, "along to the hill with it."

I sighed, but at least this bit was level. We were shielded from observation below by the houses. When we reached the left-hander on to the short hill, he edged the nose round, and as soon as the slope caught the car he sprang in and got his foot on the brake. I hoped the coil wasn't burning out. He put his head out of the window.

"They'll come after me. You follow. Not too close. If we get separated, I'll see you at your place."

117

I watched him coast down towards the river road, gathering speed. He probably had second gear in, the clutch disengaged. That's what I'd have done. But he'd know what to do. There wasn't anything he didn't know.

The engine fired just as he reached the river road. He flung the car round with screaming tyres and accelerated hard towards the waiting car, jabbing his heads on at once, to blind them I assumed. Then I ran back to the Prefect and threw myself in, my photographic wallet on the seat beside me.

This time the engine didn't start.

I cursed, jumped out, hammered the pump, and still it didn't fire. Then I realised the temperature gauge was showing warm, and I'd given it full choke. I thrust it in and tried full throttle, and it fired. As I backed round, lights went on in the semi-bungalow. The man had re-cognised his own engine on the road below.

There were headlights disappearing across the valley. They'd have to use their lights, going that fast, and to hell with concealment. I couldn't match the speed, lights or not, and they seemed to fade away before me.

I was not even sure of the route back home, and as the lights finally faded from the sky I realised I was lost. At that time, though, there was no choice of road but one, and I proceeded along it steadily, suddenly realising that the lights had appeared again, and that I was overtaking, and then that they pointed at the sky. I must have re-laxed, my brain in second gear too, because I rounded the next corner when I should have stopped and turned back. Clear in my heads was a car in a ditch, with Keele standing out on the road, waving.

There was no alternative but to keep going. I even

accelerated, and right until the last moment I believed I would run him down. Then he sprang aside and I was past, but miserably aware that although I'd kept my head down he had probably recognised the car.

I had seen no sign of a companion, Polly for instance, and Keele would surely have been reaching inside the car if he'd had an injured partner. But I felt miserable, driving away. You just cannot drive from an accident, when there could be someone injured. But now, completely submerged in illegal activities, I was in no position but to keep going. I just was not made for the sort of thing I'd become involved with.

Rather to my surprise I did not come across Comus. I'd assumed he would abandon the Alfasud and wait for me to pick him up. But there was no sign of him. I drove on, thoughtful, then found a traffic sign that made sense and headed straight for home.

It was surprising, now I came to consider it, that Keele had seemed to be alone. Comus had said that one person would not have been able to tackle both of us at the bungalow, and that seemed logical. But did that mean that a separate couple had followed us there? Two cars in silent pursuit? The follower being followed. I found that to be an idea I couldn't easily accommodate.

In any event, why had we been knocked out? What purpose had it served?

I had none of these answers when I drew the car on to my private parking patch. I could not lock it, so carefully carried all my stuff up to my rooms. Comus was not there. His lack of keys to my door did not affect my expectancy that I would find him waiting. The fact that my door was open seemed at first to confirm it.

119

"Comus?"

I put on the lights. The cat crept from beneath my easy chair. The place had been gone over.

We had been missing for hours, so there had been no hurry. But my visitor had not known that. The search had been thorough and intense. Drawers had been dragged out and left lying on the floor, their contents scattered. Cupboards had had their shelves swept clean. My bed was in a tangle on the floor, the mattress thrown in a corner. My few books were cast aside.

I ran down to the studio. Here there was also evidence of a search, but none of the chaos, possibly because there was so little in the way of a hiding place. Nothing, as far as I could see, was missing. It had been no more than a search.

This sort of thing is like a kick in the guts. In fury and in misery I climbed the stairs back to my living quarters, and for a few minutes could only sit shaking, making no attempt to restore the situation.

And then I began to worry about Comus. This was ridiculous, but I had for so long been relying on his professional expertise that I felt lost without him, and suddenly, sickeningly, afraid that he had come to some harm.

The trouble with my place is that there is no window overlooking the street, not since I blocked the light from the studio and darkroom. I wandered down to the bottom of the front staircase, opened the street door, and peered out. No sign of him. I went back up, and he was playing with the cat.

"What gives?" He waved his arm.

"I seem to have had visitors."

"Anything missing?"

"I don't think so."

"Then what secrets are you hiding that they want to know?"

"I haven't got any secrets."

"Then they're safe."

I looked at him. "I told you I hadn't got . . ." But he was eyeing me with eyebrows raised, and I realised my voice was cracking. "I expected to pick you up," I said, and lowering my voice only made it petulant.

"I watched you go by." He was picking stuff up for me, putting drawers back. "I was parked in a side road. Then I drove back."

"Why?"

"I had to check he was on his own. You can't leave an injured man . . ."

"And was he?"

"Yes." He pulled the mattress up on to the bed and began to sort out the sheets from the blankets.

"Weren't you taking a risk that he'd recognise you?"

"No. He'd know it was me, anyway. I gave him a lift to a phone box—his own radio was bust."

I exploded. "Of all the bloody stupid . . ."

"I wanted to know if they'd picked up Quayle yet."

"And he *told* you that? You chatted in the car like two old buddies . . . What did he say?"

"He said he can pick up Quayle any time. What he wants is the money—and the man in that police car who killed Quayle's men and Petar Ješić. You can see, we're both after the same thing." He turned, his eyes cold. "And you can see, in that we *are* like two old buddies."

"The money too? You want that?"

121

"Of course. Now, don't you think we ought to get down to your darkroom?"

I noticed his significant glance. I was still clasping my wallet of negatives and prints. "Soon."

"Better be quicker than that," he said. "Don't you think Keele's guessed it was you in your car? He'll be round here—"

"Oh fine. Lovely. What the hell have you brought me to? Now I'm a wanted man."

"Nonsense. Don't jitter. I've had time to get round to the Ješić̇s. There're three of our chaps scattered around here. They'll give us the tip . . ."

"So that we can make our getaway?" I demanded in despair.

"So that we can do whatever is necessary." But he was tight now, his patience running thin. "You promised me a blow-up—was that what you called it?—a blow-up of that toast shot. I got your stuff for you. So how about it?"

To be fair, that was what I had said. But the prospect of retiring to that darkroom was quite appalling, when there was no exit but the door and with a police cordon closing in on us.

"Some other time, perhaps?"

He smiled. "Now Len, now." The smile was a painful effort. It told me what it cost him in terms of retraint. It told me not to argue.

We went down into the darkroom. I flipped the wallet open on the bench and got out the negatives. They were all there, unharmed. Not even a fingerprint defiled them. I drew out the prints.

"Let's see what was so marvellous on the two that went missing."

122

They were missing out of this set, too.

I turned, bewildered. "They're not here."

"So what?"

"There'd be no *point*."

"What about that blow-up?"

"If he pinched the negatives and my proofs, and then the other two proofs from Ruźa's set, and he'd got a nice, tight safe . . ."

"The blow-up!"

"Listen! Nice tight safe that only you could open with the Encyclopaedia Britannica, then the logical thing would be to keep them together. In that case there'd be two of each of those special ones. And there're none. Comus, it's not sense."

"It's not sense to waste time." His voice grumbled with impatience. "He destroyed 'em."

"Then why not destroy the lot? Why not at least destroy those two negatives? But they're here. I know. I'd know in a second, because they're in strips, and it'd mean cutting them out of the middles . . . and recognising them . . . and a negative's a difficult thing to identify."

"Will you . . . please . . . get on . . . with it."

"I'll find those two negs for you and get a print off each."

"I shall murder you. So help me!"

"All right. All right."

Reluctantly I turned to my chemicals and dishes—there's no substitute for dishes when you're trying for a perfect print—and connected the enlarger up. I turned back and fingered through the prints again. His fists balled at his sides.

"The other's missing too," I said. "The one of you giving the toast."

"Of *course* it's bloody missing!" he shouted. "You've got it in your pocket, with the message for Quayle on the back."

Silly of me. I wasn't thinking straight. No, I was thinking too much, my heading buzzing with conjecture. But I was preparing everything precisely, long experience controlling my hands. Comus was urging me with annoying queries and generally getting underfoot.

The image of his hand was half an inch across on the original proof, which I fetched out of my pocket to use as a guide. I was reckoning to blow it up to fill a ten by eight. I switched down to amber safelight.

"That the biggest printing paper you've got?" he asked.

"No. But we only need your hand. We can do just the finger, if you like."

"Don't get stroppy."

Oh, but I felt stroppy. What could all this possibly prove?

"Don't expect too much," I warned him.

"Do it good."

"I'll need to take a few test strips. The shadows will be important."

"Do what you've got to."

He leaned against me. I felt the gun hard in my back.

"Give me room."

He watched, fascinated, as I am always still fascinated. The colours were good, and I had the gradation just right. I did a full print.

He whipped it from me, still dripping, and snapped on

124

the main light, thereby ruining a whole packet of paper I'd left open on the bench. He stared at it under the slightly swinging bulb, shadows chasing under his eyebrows.

"It's no flaming good!" he shouted. He hurled it away from him. "All that . . . for nothing."

I rescued it. As I'd told him, it's difficult to prove nothing. If there'd been a full little finger, that would have proved he'd been lying, and that somebody else had given that toast. But there was still only a space, which could have been his missing joints, or could have been a crooked finger.

"I don't know what you expected."

"This, this." He was holding up his little finger.

The healed end was not a clean, smooth dome of skin, but a knobbled mess. That, I might have captured.

"The angle was wrong," I said gently. "How'd it get like that?"

"A bullet. What's it matter?"

"I wondered why a proper job wasn't done." I stood, watching his anger. "I could try again."

He thumped my bench. Then clearly, from the street outside, I heard a shrill whistle. He met my eyes.

"There isn't time. They're here."

I stared at him, not really accepting it. Then he came close to me.

"I was *there*."

"All right, Comus."

"You don't believe me?"

"What the hell does it matter what I believe? They're here. It's all too late."

# *Ten*

He said: "Come on."

I turned away and began to get my proofs and negatives together.

"Hurry!" he called from the door.

"If you think I'm leaving . . ."

There was a hammering at my front door. A shout.

"Podmore, open up."

"Don't be fooled," said Comus. "They'll be round the back, too."

"Then . . ."

"Come *on*."

He was at the door to my landing. I joined him, my wallet hastily shuffled together, and glanced back to make sure I'd missed nothing. He ran to the head of the rear staircase, listened, then gestured upwards. I saw his lips move.

"They're here."

It was as though the words shrieked out at me. I slipped past him, edging round the newest post, and ran up to my rooms. He pressed at my heels. "Hurry, hurry."

I stopped just inside my room. He had shut the door behind us. I turned on him.

"Where the hell are we running to? They've got us trapped."

"No. There's the roof outside."

"Oh God. I'd rather . . ."

"Yes?"

I took a breath. "It's all right for you! You probably took your first steps on roofs."

He had flung open the dormer window. Eighteen inches to step up, that was all it required. He stood and regarded me steadily.

"If you've got time for clever remarks, you can't be too scared. What shoes have you got on?"

"Plastic soles."

"You'll do fine. The tiles are dry."

"Christ!"

"But stay if you'd prefer to. I don't care." He put a shoe out on to the tiles. "Thanks for trying, anyway."

Fortunately I hadn't unpacked my hold-alls. I hefted them—a fair weight—slinging them crossways over my shoulders, the weight on my hips. The wallet was under my left arm.

"I'm coming."

"Not with that lot you're not."

"Then take one for me." He hesitated. "What shoes have *you* got?"

"Leather. Here, I'll have one."

I was out beside him, standing on the grey-silver tiles. A slight breeze cut through to my skin. I peeled off one of the hold-alls.

"And the wallet," he said.

"I'll keep that."

His look was dark. I said: "I can hear them coming."

He ran from me into the moon, his feet padding confidently. The roof sloped down to my right. Dimly below

I caught a glint of glass. I moved, uneven, my left leg higher than my right. How could I possibly run? He waited, clutching a chimney. I angled up to the peak of the roof, switched the wallet to my right hand, reaching for the top edge of the tiles to steady me. Way down below, down, down, I saw the street, the tall, slim orange street lamps presenting their blank top covers to me.

My feet were slipping and skidding, my left hand painful already where I'd taken away the skin. Dust drifted into my face, and I choked.

Comus was reaching out a hand. I was above him. I tottered down the slope, throwing myself painfully behind the protection of his chimney.

He smelt of smoke.

"It's flat from here," he said, confidence in his voice. His jacket had flown open. The moon caught a glint of metal.

"Can't we just . . . hide?"

He was opening the hold-all that he was carrying over one shoulder.

"Put your wallet in here."

I had one hand steadying me behind the chimney. "No." I was here in this situation because of that wallet. To part with it now would add futility to my terror. "I'll put it in this one. And for God's sake sling that strap over your head. D'you know what you're carrying there?"

"I could replace it all in half an hour's work. This and more. Just say, and I can dump this."

I am not a basically honest man. I've bought things that I knew had fallen off a lorry, bought them and later thrown them away, because I'd found I didn't want them any more. I've tried to analyse this feeling. I have decided that the worth of things is in direct proportion to the effort you've put in earning them or producing them, and I live now by that. The contents of that hold-all represented years of painful saving. And it was all mine. What Comus could acquire in half an hour would look and feel the same, and would be new, but it would never be mine, to hold with loving pride. I'd hate it. It's nothing to do with honesty, you see.

"Dump that, Comus, and I'll dump you—over that edge. Over your head with that strap, and quick."

His face was dark. I saw no expression. His hand moved, hesitated, then unhooked the strap and lifted it over his head.

"I don't know why I trouble with you," he decided.

He had said the next bit was flat, and so it was, but it was twenty feet below. He edged down the very corner of the roof, right down to the guttering, rested his foot on it, and looked back.

"You next."

I tried to do exactly what he had done. The hold-all was now a gross weight. With every increasing second of danger it became more precious. I reached him. The guttering was creaking with his weight.

"Watch me. Do the same. I'll be below to catch you."

There was a shout behind us. A torch beam speared above our heads. I ducked. When I looked again, Comus was lowering himself over the edge, his fingers in the gutter. I choked. He released himself, and fell down into darkness. I heard his feet contact. I was sitting on the tiles, my heels wedged in the gutter.

"Drop the bag first," he called softly.

Oh no, no. He'd miss it.

"I can see you against the sky," he said, apparently reading my mind.

I lifted the strap over my head and hung the bag over the edge. With agony I released it. There was no crash. I sighed.

"Now you."

And I had no alternative, now that everything I really owned was down there with him. I rolled over on to my stomach and slowly, fingers painfully gripping the jutting edges of the tiles, I lowered myself beyond the guttering, feeling it play its agonising edge up my shins, legs, body, until there was nothing left of me but my hands, and those without feeling, so tight were they clamped on that wavering lip. The cat came and peered with disapproval over the edge at me.

"Let go."

What else could I do? Perhaps my toe caught the wall on the way down. I felt I was not falling straight, was toppling over backwards. Then I was in his arms, had sent him cursing on to his back, and my leg was doubled beneath me.

"You only had to come straight down," he complained, scrambling to my side.

"My ankle!"

"What have you done?"

"I think it's broken."

"If it was, you wouldn't think, you'd know." He put a hand beneath my arm. "Try standing on it."

I did. "Oh God!"

"The next bit's easy."

"I've heard that before."

"You're doing great. There's a roof light over there."

130

"I can't . . . walk . . . on it."

"Try." He urged me forward.

"My cameras!"

He swore violently. Then he said quietly: "I'll get 'em."

He swung both bags over his shoulders, carefully cross-shouldered so as not to incite my wrath. Leaning against the wall, I tried a little weight on my ankle. Pain blinded me.

"You'd better leave me here."

"Oh lovely." He laughed bitterly. "They might never find you. You'd starve to death. The pigeons'd strip your bones clean."

"Send 'em a postcard. Tell 'em where I am."

"That's better. Your old flippant self. Let's give it a try."

We made it to the roof light, which was an eight foot by four horizontal area of glass like a garden frame. "Soon have this open," he said. But strangely he had trouble with it.

"What's up?" Where's your technique?"

"Things can stick. Here, have these bloody bags a minute."

Without them, bracing his legs and hooking his fingers under the edge, he applied himself to the problem. It came up with a crack.

"Technique," he said, and re-arranged my hold-alls without a word from me. He leaned over and put his head inside. He seemed a long time. When he raised his head he murmured: "Have to give your eyes time. It's a storeroom. If I go first, you might not be able to make it. I'll drop you."

I hissed with pain at the thought.

"How far?"

"Nine feet at the most. With both our arms at full stretch, there'll be no more than two feet."

"All right."

With almost no help from me he lifted me over the edge until I was again suspended by my hands. He took my wrists, on his knees by the opening, and then gradually lowered me until he was face down, the edge of the frame cutting into his throat. Accordingly, he could say nothing in warning. He simply let me go.

I fell on the good foot and rolled clear, away from the bad one. Because I hadn't howled, he knew I was safe, and in a second he was beside me.

"You OK?"

"I think so." I shuffled, getting my good foot under me. "No, I want to try by myself."

Because of this, he was against the wall at the time, and I was in the middle of the room. That breeze which had cut through me must have freshened. He had left the hinged roof light in a vertical position. With a creak it moved. I had a chance to glance up, and saw it swinging down under its own weight.

It fell with a crash into its frame and one of the panes shattered. Glass showered down around me. Then silence.

"Len, Len."

I was holding my breath on a scream. He sensed it and dived for the wall, his hand scrabbling for a lightswitch. It blinded me.

"Not . . . the light," I gasped.

"After that, what does it matter?" He bent over me.

132

"Let me see."

A shaft of glass had sliced down my arm from shoulder to elbow, ripping through my denim jacket like a seam tearing apart. I had my right hand clamped over it and could already feel the blood warm through my fingers. There was no pain yet, just the teeth-chilling agony of the thought of it.

"Jacket off," he snapped, peeling himself out of my hold-alls. He gently helped my left arm out of the remnants of the sleeve. I could barely bear to look.

It was a deep gash about four inches long, blood streaming from it. He removed my jacket, and with savage strength tore it top to bottom into strips.

"Not hygienic," he said, binding them round my arm. "We'll have to get you to a doctor."

"The one you took your pinkie to?" I bit my lip.

"It'll hurt," he told me pleasantly. "I think we'd better call the cops."

"No."

"You can't get much further."

"Pick my bags up."

"Your ankle . . ."

"It's the principle of needle therapy. One pain disperses the other. My ankle's great. Where to now, buster?"

It was just that I'm stubborn. I wasn't going to shout for help, when he would have scorned it. He helped me to my feet. Oh, the ankle was fine, no more than a burning warning not to be too clever. My head swam. Apart from that . . .

"Put the light out," I said, and he helped me from the door.

133

We were in the attic of an office block, dirty rotting wooden stairs at the top, then linoleum, then carpet, and finally polished grano-marble, down which we left a run of blood spots. We were in the vestibule, double glass doors leading to the street. Orange light slanted in. Two police cars occupied the yellow lines outside.

"A few words on their radio," he said, "and they'd get an ambulance here."

"Try the back."

We found our way out into a rear yard full of boxes of shredded confidence, from there into an alleyway. Here all was dark. This was a maze of connecting alleys in the centre of the block complex.

"Where're we heading?" It was only a matter of putting one foot in front of the other, I found. That, and continuing to do so.

"Away," he said. "Hold on." He leaned me against a wall. A dustbin lid rattled against my thigh. "You're shivering."

"A bit cold."

"The shock."

He disentangled himself from my bags and peeled off his jacket. This was a quality worsted he was wearing, not too perfect by that time. He shrugged my arms through the sleeves. It hung baggy, like an overcoat. He took up my hold-alls again.

"Not much further."

It was all part of his training, an infallible sense of direction and a mental map of the town. We came out behind the Town Hall.

I had been vaguely aware for some time of activity all around us. Police car sirens called to the night, subdued it seemed, as though they had a gentler siren for people who slept. Slept at night? Weren't they lucky! There were a few calling voices and running feet. No whistles. Have you noticed that—they don't use whistles these days. A great pity, I think. There was an urgency about the shrill call of a copper's whistle. It added to their image of efficiency. Now they stick radios to their faces, and the effect is as inspiring as a pop singer trying to stick his lollipop down his throat.

"Hold on there," said Comus. "Can't have you passing out now. There's the Landrover."

It sat, the other side of the street, waiting and beckoning in the Borough Engineer's slot. At that time of night it was naked in the empty run behind the Town Hall.

"Now," said Comus, and somehow I made it across the street. Police winkers were everywhere. I couldn't see how they missed us.

There was a piece of paper under the wiper blade. Comus tore it free and threw it at me. By that time he had me in the passenger's seat. I read it from the light above the Mayor's slot.

"If you want to use my parking space, apply for planning permission."

It was an in-joke I couldn't understand. I puzzled over it all the way through the centre of town.

Apparently it all depends on nerve. You drive as though you have a right, something not withdrawn from you by illegal activities. You even rasp the horn impatiently if a squad car bars your way. You shout out of the window, demanding information. Comus did that. I was too far gone to do any more than nod vaguely as we passed. And pass we did, clear through the pack of them

135

and their now-abortive search, and headed out to the Ješićs'.

I suppose it must have been around four in the morning. Not so many cars occupied the square parking patch. As we drew in, Comus gave a code signal on his horn, and by the time he'd got round to my side they had the front door open, light streaming out.

I had an impression of Jovan Ješić waving and flapping, of his wife fluttering in distress, and Ruža's face, her eyes . . .

"In the kitchen," she said softly. Her breath was sweet on my face. I tried to walk. Comus was one side of me, Danny Summers the other, Ljubica twittering in front and tripping over the edge of her nightie. They got me down on a chair at the long table, a bowl of steaming, fresh-smelling water beside me, and first-aid equipment mounting in front of me. I had a vague idea that they'd done this before, and that they'd be capable of removing the odd bullet or two from my person, not perhaps without pain, but efficiently.

Ruža was clearly in charge of this aspect of their normal life. She swivelled the chair so that my arm was unobstructed. She had rolled her nightdress sleeves right up to her shoulders, and was directing the removal of Comus's jacket, which they dumped on the table at my right hand.

"It needs stitches," she said.

"Can't you just . . ."

"Now you be quiet."

Her lips were set. No hint of her humour now in their firm line, nor in her deep, dark eyes. Her face was naked for the night. No make-up contributed to the curve or

136

colour of her mouth. I wanted to kiss those lips, just to confirm that the taste would be natural, but she turned away and began to cut plaster into short strips.

Comus had not relaxed. Previously, driving, I had seen him so, but experience had taught me that he relaxes at the full stretch of his reactions. Now he lounged, a blurred face moving beyond all their nodding, muttering heads, his only hint of strain being a sudden desire for a cigarette. He flapped at pockets that were not there, and as I like to be helpful I reached with my free hand for the jacket beside me.

He dived. There was a cry of surprise, and Ljubica staggered aside.

"I'll get . . ." I began.

But my hand had found the wrong pocket, his inside breast pocket, and what it came out with, blood-stained but not completely spoiled, was three of my own wedding proofs, one of the toast that had led to this awkward situation, one of the groom and best man arriving at the church, and one of that early group, with the fake copper grinning in the background.

# Eleven

The steaming bowl went skittering from the table. I was on my feet. Ruźa cried out, because her fingers had torn the wound open again. Blood spattered down the front of her nightgown.

But I had seen in one glance what I had dismally failed to recall from my memory, that the fake policeman had been Comus himself. And instantly, on that knowledge, which had been denied me with such effort, I knew the truth.

"No . . ." he roared, reaching. But he saw it was too late. His hand fell, and he was still.

But I was raging, completely beyond self-control because I was too weak to make the effort of restraint.

"It was *you* pinched my negatives!" I shouted.

I saw it all, as a complete picture, with the clarity of delirium. I tried to express it, whirling my arms wildly when anyone tried to touch me. Jeśić was frozen, his face hard. Ruźa appealed at my shoulder, plucking at me in protest at my distress. But she could not have understood my disillusionment, nor have realised how close in trust I had come to Comus. My bitter anger rejected her. I saw the pity in her eyes, and threw it back at her with the words I aimed at Comus. Blood dripped from my fingertips.

"Oh, you were clever. I didn't know you and the copper were the same person, so you had to keep me not

138

knowing. Because then I'd see how you used that car after all, as planned, *their* fake copper." I whirled my arms wildly, indicating the total group. Them! The enemy. They had me there at their mercy, and I railed against them in commuted agony. "You only had to take your blasted navy blue jacket off, and you'd be ready to jump . . . jump in the soddin' car."

I faltered. I lost it, then. The outrage blurred the fine clarity of the image.

"Len . . . Len . . ."

I tried to get over the table at him, but fell back. "And the two proofs . . . the proofs . . ."

What was it about the proofs? I couldn't find it in the jungle of my emotions.

"It doesn't mean I—"

"But yes, you. It had to be. I nearly had it at one time. What was . . . yes, the fact that it wasn't important what had been taken, but what was left. God, Comus, how you've cheated me on that!"

He shook his head, pain in his eyes, but I plunged on. "I didn't see right through it. No, Ruźa . . . please . . ." I couldn't find it in me to use violence to free her fingers. "He's going to hear."

The fact was that, without those two early prints, each with his face on, anybody looking at the set remaining couldn't say *who* had been missing later. It had been a simplification to send the toast picture to Quayle and ask where Comus had been after the bank job, because Quayle knew who was meant. Quayle had known who'd been the best man. But someone not knowing that—the police for instance—could search the set I'd given them, less the critical two, and not realise that anybody was

139

missing, because there was not one picture in there that featured the best man. And because they could not see him, they could not know he should be there.

*That* was the reason the two prints were stolen, to hide from the police the fact of Comus's absence at the time the Quayle men were being shot, the money taken from their car—and Petar Ješić removed because he knew too much by that time.

That much was crystal clear in my head, but I couldn't get it into words. I blubbered and stammered, and fell back into the chair, and only disconnected phrases emerged as the ideas chased themselves through my mind.

"Your bungalow . . . it was yours." His own place, we had burgled. "How clever to know the combination." And to knock me out while he took from the set the three prints that mattered. "It was all a con!" I screamed at him, as Jovan held me down in the chair. "No blow-up of that hand was going to prove you were there at the . . . the reception. Because you weren't."

Details coursed their way through my memory, Comus kidding me he'd got the combination from the encyclopaedias, Comus using Quayle's intervention to prove to me that he was offering that toast. And Comus so good with a gun!

I was whimpering, I knew. My eyes were on the table now, because I could not look him in the face.

"But why me? Why, Comus?"

I turned to Ruźa, amazed at the idea. All of it had been to persuade *me*. Not specifically the police—me! "Ruźa," I whispered, "why did it have to be for me?"

But she was not listening, not understanding probably. She was bent in concentration over my arm. My violence had broken it free again. I turned away as she glanced once into my eyes, unable to face the blinding pity, and Ljubica stood at my elbow with a small glass.

"Drink this." Again the pity, her eyes almond and calm.

"No."

Because I still wanted to think. Because there was something beyond it.

"Drink," Ljubica whispered. "It'll help."

It was bitter. I choked it down, eager for anything that would help. I was aware that Comus had seized my hold-alls and was tearing them open. I protested feebly. He was venting his spite . . . I raised an arm, but it was heavy. He had my wallet. By what I had said, I was dreamily aware, I had betrayed him to his friends. But that could not be so—they must already know. It made no sense . . . I had just told them he had killed Ruźa's brother . . . yet they'd have to know that, too. So why was he trying to destroy the evidence . . .

He scattered prints on the table.

"Ruźa, stop him," I whispered.

Then he found what he wanted, reached forward and selected one of the three I had found in his pocket, and by its side he slapped its duplicate from my wallet.

I could not focus. The room was receding, the voices softer. Then my eyes cleared, and I was looking at two identical prints of the best man toasting the bridesmaids. They were the two original proofs, not from the degraded copies I'd made for Ruźa.

I blinked, and they faded, ran together, and I plunged down into effortless sleep, still reaching for the peace I

141

had left behind, and Comus's voice: "I know, Len, I know."

When I awoke I was in a narrow bed in a small, plain room. A man I did not know was sitting watching me. Seeing my eyes open, he went immediately to the door and called out down the stairs. Then Ljubica came to me, with her father.

There had been a few minutes between the shout and their appearance. During this time I tried to recover my scattered wits, but there was too much in the tangle, and my strange companion could not or would not help me. I could see no sign of my equipment, and this distressed me almost more than my arm, which felt as though I would never be able to hold a camera to my eye again.

"Now lie still," said Ljubica.

Jovan Ješić eyed me severely. He put his hands on his hips and tilted his head, then reached up and pulled one end of his moustache. He nodded. It was a signal to Ljubica.

"Let me see," she said.

She meant the arm. They had not stitched it, but had drawn the edges together with plaster, and a very neat job it was too. But tender! If she breathed on it I nearly shot from the bed.

"You'll live."

There was a look in her eyes that said I'd better, because perhaps she was growing tired of Danny Summers, and fancied someone with a more restful occupation than robbing banks, or whatever his part was in the set-up. I smiled to myself at the thought. She gave me a couple of tablets to swallow.

"Comus says you're too tough to die," she whispered.

142

Was it a compliment? Comus? I tried to lean up.

"Where is he?"

"Gone away. Now be good. We can't have you spoiling things now."

All double-meaning stuff you'll have realised. What things?

"Your arm, silly." Perhaps I'd spoken aloud. She leaned forward and kissed me on the forehead. "Be good." Then she left, her duties completed.

The other man, who might have been another Ješić—seeing that Jovan referred to him as son—took a position with his back against the door, I felt as a guard. I was in no condition to take any violent action.

"Marko will watch over you," said Jovan.

"I'm not about to make a break for it."

He smiled, drew up a wooden kitchen chair and sat beside me, placing his big hands on his knees. "Who can be certain with you? No, it's for you he's there. The majority decision was to kill you and have done with it."

I thought about that. The idea was difficult to accept.

"You're not the majority?"

He shrugged. "It's the fate of most family businesses these days. They grow. I was a fool, I admit. Stick to your craft, that's what I always say—and not do. The Ješićs had a tradition. We were known throughout the country. Visit any police station and ask about delicacy of operation, ask them about careful planning and smooth execution, with not a bruise left behind, and they'll speak of the Ješićs with awe."

"I'm sure you're very proud," I murmured. I could have done with a cup of tea.

143

"And admiration," he said, his eyes glazed with self-approval.

"But you expanded?"

"Outsiders!" He scowled. "They follow us like a cloud of gnats."

"Such as Comus and Martin?"

"Ruźa married poorly."

"Seven times."

"There was no fibre to him. No staying power."

"Anybody'd get fed up with that. Seven times to different women, that I could understand . . ."

"It amuses you to be flippant," he said severely.

I blushed. There had been criticism of Ruźa in what I'd said.

"I'd be proud to marry your daughter, sir. Seven times . . . a dozen."

"I wasn't looking for recruits."

"No. I'm sorry. You were saying that you already had too many."

"Comus . . ."

"Betrayed you?"

"Comus held us together. Comus was the son I wished I'd had." He glanced at Marko in brief apology, and the lad shrugged. "He's been my lieutenant for five years. I'd have trusted him with my life. I have, several times."

A shadow crossed his eyes. Then he turned and made a sudden gesture, and Marko left the room.

"Aren't you afraid to be left alone with me?" I asked. "I'm violent."

His mouth twitched, but he treated it as another pleasantry.

"Martin betrayed us to Quayle," he said.

144

"Comus told me that."

"What should have been a clean job, perfect in every detail, came out as a murderous botch in Quayle's hands. It's a matter of pride. I wouldn't want anybody to think it was the work of the Jeśićs."

"Nobody believes that," I said comfortingly. My arm was throbbing and my mouth dry. Where was that tea?

"But they would, with *my* policeman on one of your pictures, and my car on another."

"Yours?"

"For a short while. To be returned—the car."

"Yes. So Comus stole my negatives, and you all hid the two proofs from Ruźa's set."

"Comus stole your wallet, yes. We do not know who took the two proofs." I moved to protest, but he held up his hand. "I told you, there are hangers-on, light-fingered rubbish I shall shortly dismiss. But for now . . . they remain, because we do not yet know who."

"Oh, come on . . . Comus took 'em."

He shook his head. "What you say is impossible—that he left with the car and my son Petar. That he shot Quayle's men—so much I could accept—but that he should kill Petar . . . No! For the money, he'd kill Petar? Never. In any event, Comus was at the reception at the time."

"Which we cannot prove."

"Do we need to prove it? Only the family matters in this, and we know he was at the reception."

"It must be expensive, all those receptions." It was a stray thought, a kind of refuge from what I should have been thinking.

"I was the missing one," he said quietly.

145

"What!"

He smiled. "Oh, not me in the car. Your imagination runs on fantasies. I drove to Beatings and visited Quayle. It was a good time for it. He'd be alone there, waiting . . ."

"I thought he was at the bank."

"Minnit and Carraway, yes, and that idiot youth. And two men for the getaway with the money. Quayle's past it. He can't control his hands—but you'll have seen. He waits at home and sweats over the phone. He was alone when I got there. We talked. At that time I knew only that my plans had been betrayed, and he had not heard that he'd lost two men and the money. So we were both reasonable. There was no . . . animosity. He told me who had tipped him off. Martin. But I'd suspected it. You'll understand, though, that you can't move without confirmation."

"Of course not."

"Quayle was agreeable that I should do it. After all, I was saving him a cut."

"Of what he hadn't got?"

"What he didn't get." The thought comforted him. "He'd be furious—that he'd let me have Martin, and for nothing."

You had to keep talking, that was the trick, otherwise you'd go mad. "Comus knows?"

"He suspects, I believe. At the moment it suits him to say it was Quayle killed his brother."

"But he'd like as not to go out and blow Quayle's head off!"

"No great loss," he said absently.

"Or blow off yours when he finds out." I was trying to

146

shake him. He did not respond. "When I tell him."

"No." He shook his head, not, apparently, that I wouldn't be able to tell Comus. "No, he owes me one. For Petar."

"Where's your damned logic!" I shouted, and pain shot clear to my fingertips. "You said it wasn't him in that car."

"But he *should* have been," he said reprovingly. "It was indefensible in my lieutenant, fooling about and trying to get in on the groups. He's vain, that one, and he can't keep his hands off Ljubica."

"Vain! I thought he was shy."

"Not him." He thought about it. "He poses for those secret cameras they've got in the banks these days."

I lay back and absorbed it. Like Vitamin C, it drains through, given time.

"Why are you telling me this?" I asked weakly to the ceiling.

"Because I want you to know the truth."

"To carry to my grave, I suppose?" But not seriously. They'd hardly repair me and feed me with truths—if nothing else—if I was destined for early extinction.

"I've said you're safe—if you remain here quietly." It was his word, his bond. And for some reason I felt I could trust this strange old man with his twisted morality.

He slapped his knees with that finality visitors have at the bedside of the sick. I said quickly:

"And Ruźa?"

He was on his feet. "She's well."

"You know damn well what I mean."

"She was upset at Martin's death, of course. But it was a poor marriage. He was . . . unsatisfactory. Ruźa is a

147

warm girl. Takes after her momma," he said dreamily. "It takes a man . . . But you know what they say, marry in haste . . ."

"Seven times is a lot of leisure."

"Seven times the error is compounded. I'll leave you now."

They can walk away, sick visitors, when they've had their say. I called after him: "Wait!"

He paused in the doorway. Marko was lounging at the stairhead beyond him.

"One thing doesn't make sense," I told him. He came back inside. His face was expressionless. "One thing . . . that police car. A stranger got into it, but you don't know who. Yet it got back to where you had it from."

"Martin had the gate keys. That was why he worked there."

"No. Martin might have betrayed your plans to Quayle. But someone else got in that car with your son, and it wasn't one of your people. It wasn't one of Quayle's either. So your plans must have been betrayed twice, Jovan. Once to Quayle, and once to someone else, who was going to get the drop on both of you. Do you think that second betrayer was also Martin? It wouldn't make sense. There's another person, Jovan, and you know it."

Not a muscle moved on his face. "I told you, someone took the two proofs." Not a muscle but his talking ones.

"The same one?"

"We shall find out." He turned again to leave.

"But Jovan." He looked back. "The car got to where it came from. And you must have known it would, because you took Martin's body there and left it inside."

"Ruža will bring you something to eat."

"I'm not that hungry. It can wait. You said I had to know the truth."

He smiled, shaking his head in defeat. "You're a hard man."

"The truth . . ."

"I didn't take Martin there. I left his body on the police station steps."

He got out before I could think of anything to follow that. After a minute I got it, sat upright, and shouted:

"Then how the hell did he get to the car . . ."

Ruža chose that moment to enter with a tray. There was no sign of Marko, so I guessed he *had* been Ješić's protector. Flattering, I suppose.

Ruža smiled. "We *are* getting excited, aren't we!"

She wasn't. Placid, that's the word. No . . . impersonal. The smile was professional.

"Have you ever been a nurse?"

"Trainee. Only for a couple of months. We needed an ambulance for a job . . ."

"Never mind."

"Can you manage scrambled eggs on toast? And tea and scones and cake?"

I realised, then, that it was evening, and I must have lost about twelve hours. My watch had stopped.

"I've been out for twelve hours?"

She put the tray on the table beside the bed. "Thirty-six," she said. "Ljubica's rather casual with her doses."

"Then don't let her get near me again."

"She won't be. Here, I'll get this pillow behind your shoulders. That better? Can you use a knife and fork?"

"The fork anyway. You do the cutting."

149

She was in a practical, plain outfit of dark, wrap-over skirt and a white sweater. It was a pleasure watching her doing the cutting. I realised I'd never seen her in slacks of jeans.

"Is my stuff safe?" I asked.

"Yes. Downstairs. Can you manage now?"

"I think so. And my car?"

"It's outside."

Somebody must have fetched it. But . . . considering the police would be looking for it . . . "Parked?"

"Of course. Now . . . if you're all right."

"Don't go."

"There are things to do."

"Stay and talk."

"Don't you know it all yet? I thought you were so clever."

I ignored her tone. "Where's Comus?"

"He said he had business. He doesn't confide in me."

Then she left. Abruptly.

Considering she'd entered with a smile, her short visit had not been inspiring. After I'd eaten all I could I lay and thought. Then, because thinking was apt to lead me into trouble, I looked round for something to read, but the room was almost completely bare and I could see nothing to distract me. When I listened, I realised that the house was singularly quiet, when it usually contained the teaming tribes of Ješić and his followers. I wondered whether I should bang the floor, but then decided it might attract the attention of those who'd voted for my death.

I decided to look at the sunset. The sun was low and was slanting through the window, orange across the bare boards of the floor. The window was the other side of the room.

It was when I attempted to reach it that I recalled that an ankle was involved, too. That and my weakness . . . But once you start a thing, it's best to finish it. I got to the window. She had said my car was outside. There it was, and it was alone. There was no other vehicle, no square parking patch, but a cobbled, muddied farm yard with broken-down barns opposite me and an old plough in the field behind, and beyond the field an immense disappearing of valley, fading into the grey and purple slopes of distant mountains.

I was certainly not in the Ješić Victorian mansion.

By moving round the wall I managed to reach the door. It was locked. I hammered on it and shouted, and then there were running feet on bare wooden stairs. I stood back, tottering. The door flew open and Danny Summers came in. Marko lurked on the landing.

"Oh Christ, he's come to life," said Danny.

He was holding a gun in his hand.

I was becoming generally bored with guns. It seemed that nobody could get anything done without a gun in his hand. The modern disease. If they picked up a spade instead . . .

"Are you holding me?" I asked, a little loudly I admit.

"Oh Lord, didn't he tell you before he left? You're recuperating. Out of harm's way."

"What harm?"

"Where Quayle can't reach you, and the police can't. . ."

"You're protecting me?"

"Sort of."

151

"Then why do it with a gun pointed at my belly? It's habit, that's what it is. You people make me sick. Do you stir your tea with it?"

Danny wasn't perhaps too bright. He looked sheepish and stuck it in his belt.

"Now get back into bed and behave yourself," he said, trying to recover the initiative.

"I've just spent a day and a half in bed."

Then Ruźa came to investigate the trouble, and as she, being my medical adviser at that time, could see no reason why I should remain there if I was going to be difficult about it, they eventually helped me into what clothes I'd got left and down the stairs into the long, low living room, where we could all sit amicably and watch Coronation Street. By all, I mean Ruźa and myself, Danny and Marko. Jovan and Ljubica had disappeared.

And the two stalwarts had, really, had no sleep, and dozed off in their chairs.

"How long," I asked, "am I going to be kept here?"

She got up to turn down the sound. "Until you're fit."

"No. Something's going on. I'm being kept out of the way."

"There are things to be sorted out."

"Where's Comus?"

She looked away. She had her hair short, deep chestnut hair, I'd decided, not black. The line of her neck, with her head turned away, was delightful.

"He's got business with Quayle."

"About Martin?"

"Yes."

"That's a lie." Her eyes flashed, but I continued. "Quayle didn't kill Martin."

"No?" Her voice was toneless.

"It's about your brother, isn't it? Petar. I remember . . . the last few seconds . . . Comus said he knew."

"I don't know what Comus could have had in mind."

I got up and turned off the picture, remaining standing, facing her. "I think he knows who was in that car with your brother, and who killed him."

She stood up abruptly, agitatedly. "Oh, I'm tired of your words . . . words . . ."

"Don't you want to know, too?"

"Yes. Of course, you fool." Then she was angry. "You accused Comus of doing that."

"I was furious, and blind. I see now that I got it wrong."

"Comus said you were like that." She was bitterly scornful, resenting the fact that I was like that. "Always knows, he said. Big-headed. First you're sure you're right, then you're just as sure you were wrong."

"Wrong in a way of looking at it."

"Ah yes, not conceding too much, are you!"

"I said he'd taken the two prints out of your set to hide the fact that he'd not been at the reception."

"He *was* there."

"To hide the fact that he'd apparently not been at the reception? That better? But . . . who was he hiding it from, Ruźa? That's the point. Not from your lot, that's a fact, because you all swear he was there. You've just said it again. And not from Quayle, because he couldn't care tuppence for what Quayle thinks. And when it came to it, the picture that triggered Quayle wasn't one of those two at all, it was the one of the bridesmaid's toast. That leaves the police—but Comus had covered himself there

153

by stealing my wallet and proofs, and it was just not reasonable to suppose that the police could go round to your place and ask for *your* proofs, and expect to get 'em. No, Ruźa, it wasn't for the benefit of *any* of them. So who does that leave? Well, there's me. Old big-head himself."

This thought I had grappled with, and could find no way round. I was appealing to her. Why? Why?

"You're doing well," she murmured, and why then was she so disturbed?

"You're not going to help me?"

She turned away. In their chairs the slumberers stirred.

"But if it was me," I went on, "if I was the only one being fooled, as I seem to have been all along, why would Comus have needed to extract *both* the prints? Extracting both from that set, I'll agree, has stopped me from recognising Comus as your fake copper. That was all he wanted to do, because at that time there was real suspicion that the fake policeman *had* been in that car, and that therefore your father's crowd had retaliated against Quayle by homing the police in on their car."

"But Petar was dead!" she cried from the heart.

"There was always the possibility that Quayle's men had fought back, and Petar got killed in the . . ."

"They were getaway men, un-armed."

"I didn't know that."

"I . . . I! It's always you."

"Isn't it? Me who has to be fooled. And in the end I fooled myself. If Comus had intended to continue to hide his identity as the fake copper from *me*, then he'd only have needed to take one print from your set, Ruźa,

154

the one with that copper on. But both went, and me, stupid and wild because he'd been covering himself, I thought he'd taken both. But why should he? The disappearance of both, by a process of inversion and by considering what was left behind, told me that he was covering his absence from the reception. It *told* me that. Why should Comus do such a thing? Of course he wouldn't. Somebody else took them."

"We already know that."

"But it's me who has to be convinced. Haven't you realised that? They were taken deliberately to frame him. For my benefit, Ruźa."

"Oh, you're impossible."

"There's something you're hiding."

"Something you are. Pretending, anyway. This is another bluff. You persist in it." Her lips were almost colourless with passion. She hated me for persisting.

"There's no bluff now, and I'm rotten at poker. I've got nothing to cover."

"Len . . . please!"

I think I'd have got it then. I was about to protest, but she suddenly raised her arm. I was silent. She ran quickly to the window. Then she snapped out: "Marko! Danny!" The authority was there. They jumped awake.

"A car," she said.

I stood beside her at the window. The car rocked down a rutted approach, which was no more than two grooves beaten by car tyres. There was dust whipped up behind it, the lowering sun bronzing it. He approached, and drew to a halt behind my Prefect.

"It's all right," I said. "It's only Keele."

155

# Twelve

I was so immersed in the idea that every thought and action around there was directed towards me that I instantly assumed he had brought a warrant for my arrest. He climbed out of his car. I saw that he was alone.

"Marko, out the back. Get round behind him. Danny, you stay by the door. You." Ruźa glared at me. "Stay put."

"He can't touch me."

"He wants to take you away."

"So I assumed. But he can't . . ."

"I don't want him to."

I smiled at her. She tossed her head. "Damn you," she whispered. Then she went to the door, opened it, and stood out in the yard.

"Don't come any nearer," she called.

"Is this your hospitality?" he asked, pleasant, easy. But his mouth was hard.

"Would you welcome *me*?"

"Any time, my dear, at the station. But it's Podmore I want."

"He isn't here."

I thrust past Danny and to the door. It was ridiculous that he would come all this way—wasn't this Wales?—and alone, simply to pick me up.

"He's right behind you," said Keele.

I saw her shoulders stiffen. Then her words were for

me, though she did not take her eyes from Keele.

"Go with him, if that's what you want."

"If I was guilty of anything, then I'd go, if only to save you from shooting·him. But I'm not. All I've done is help a man burgle his own home. Nothing illegal there."

And yet there was a slight quickening of fear. Keele was clearly confident.

"We've received a complaint from Quayle," he said severely.

"Quayle?"

"That you assaulted him and his friends. That you blinded Carraway . . ."

"Ridiculous."

"Well, he can't see."

"It was only photographic bleach. He'll see if he opens his eyes."

"That you fired a weapon at Cornelius Minnit . . ."

"Self defence. And I missed."

"And that you intimidated Quayle himself by firing a shotgun at him."

"He was reaching for a gun."

"I've no information about that. I am charging you, Leonard Patrick Podmore, in that . . ."

"This is bloody stupid," I shouted. "Can you see that lot in a witness box!"

I might not have spoken. "I also have a complaint from a Mr and Mrs Albright, that you blasted a hole in a darkroom door, thereby rendering it completely unsuitable for its designed purpose . . ."

"For God's sake!"

"And that you did then blast a similar hole in a Persian

carpet valued at £2,000, rendering that equally . . ."

"What's the matter with you!"

"And that you did then assault Mrs Albright."

"What!"

"In that you . . ."

"Cut out the fancy talk," I howled.

"She said you kissed her, when she was incapable of defending herself."

"Did you come all the way here with that load of rubbish?"

"There is also the matter of assistance in the theft of a car, to wit, one Alfasud . . ."

"You can't be serious!"

"Serious enough to swear a warrant and draw a weapon." He produced it. "Knowing that I'd meet armed opposition."

I was out of words. I gasped. Ruźa said: "Hadn't you better go with him?"

I was surprised at the sarcasm in her tone. "What's the matter with you all?"

She turned. The pain in her eyes was crippling. "It's sufficient excuse. A load of rubbish, but an excuse. You can go now. All honour saved . . ."

"What the hell is going on around here?" I demanded.

"If you persist," she said miserably.

"I'm not going with him! Weren't you supposed to protect me?"

"Not if it's only to go on with the pretence." Her head was high now. Dignity hardened her face. I didn't like that dignity.

"Send the bugger packing," I said angrily.

Keele had produced the stubby revolver only to

demonstrate that he was armed. But now his hand closed more firmly around the butt, and he made a gesture with it that angered me; there was a peremptory arrogance in it.

"Get your stuff," he said, "and put it in your car."

Marko had been moving gradually from a point where I had first spotted him, beyond the far barn. I could see what he was aiming at, the wreck of a tractor, which, if he could reach it, would place him squarely behind Keele, and at the same time with some protection.

"You can't force me to bring anything," I said firmly, but I was aware at once that I had conceded the possibility that he could force me to go without. Ruźa glanced at me. Her mouth expressed a shade of disgust.

"String it on," she said softly. "But not too far."

"I don't know what you mean."

"If you're intending to go anyway, please don't involve Danny and my brother in shooting." So cold . . .

I reached towards her to protest. Keele saw the movement and stiffened. Ruźa glanced from one to the other of us, and gave a flat little laugh.

Suddenly, Danny stepped forward and beside me. His advance seemed at first a hint of aggression, but his words, in that event, countered it. "Please . . . Sergeant."

And Keele drew back his head with a snort of disgust.

It was at that moment that Marko made his move across the final ten yards of open ground. Keele, his head raised in that second, just caught the movement in the corner of his eye. He twisted round quickly, crouching, but Marko dived for cover and made it before Keele, if he'd intended, could fire.

I had thought Ruźa's skirt to be neat and practical. I now saw why she favoured it to jeans. Nowhere in skin-tight jeans could she have hidden a pistol, but the skirt was a simple wrap-around with an overlap. From somewhere in there she produced a small pistol, in the moment of Keele's diverted attention. I thought she intended to fire it, but instead she thrust it into my hand. It was warm.

"Use it, if you want to stay."

If that was amusement I saw in her eyes, it was at my complete and blank sense of loss. I stood like a fool with it in my hand, not pointing it, not even certain whether she would have kept it where it had been without its safety catch on.

"Right," said Keele. "Right. That's resisting arrest."

"Now look . . ." I showed it to him, then approached a couple of paces. "I don't even know if the safety's on. Is it? I mean—you'd know."

"Stop!" he called out. I stopped. "Take one more step and I fire. Drop the gun at your feet, and then approach slowly."

I half turned away. "You said I could get my stuff."

Then I simply stood. Somehow, I realised, there was a test going on here; of me, of Ruźa, of Keele? I didn't know. Keele was frowning at the immensity of his problem—Marko behind him, Danny facing him, and me in the middle. And Ruźa . . .

"Now, Len, now!" she suddenly cried. "Between the eyes."

"I'm sorry." How does one apologise for not murdering a man? "I don't really know how."

160

Keele's smile was grim. "You," he said to Ruźa, "turn slowly and go back inside. Get his stuff, all of it, and let me see you come out with one bag in each hand. And if . . . if that maniac behind me tries one shot, I swear to you *he* gets it first." He jerked the gun expressively at Danny, and glared coldly. "And Marko gets it next. I know Marko couldn't hit a barn."

Then behind me Danny whispered: "You wouldn't do that, Sergeant!"

Would he not? His eyes told a different story.

Ruźa moved. Marko laughed gleefully—in truth, he was a maniac—and in order to prove his marksmanship fired at the barn. Sheer high-spirits, but it sparked Keele's nerves, and the nothing at the end of his gun suddenly centred on Danny's chest. I was half turning, attracted by Ruźa's move, and saw the sudden terror on Danny's face. He flung his arms wide, as though to demonstrate his lack of resistance but unfortunately he did not release his gun. I could see that Keele would fire. So what else could I do but squeeze that trigger, and just in case the pistol jerked upwards I lifted its angle to be certain the shot missed him.

Ruźa threw herself at my legs. I felt myself going, automatically trying to favour my bad arm, and Marko went wild, my shot having smacked into the barn door only a foot above his head. He fired rapidly three times, and dust flew at Keele's feet. He turned and ran for his car and Marko gave a whoop of delight, coming out into the open and crouching, two hands to the gun now, steadying it for the one that mattered.

"No!" I howled, wriggling in Ruźa's arms.

Danny cried out something. He ran past me.

"Sergeant . . ."

Perhaps he intended to divert Marko's attention. Nobody wants a dead policeman. He stumbled, and Marko yelled: "Leave him!"

But Danny recovered. He ran straight at the car, and Keele paused, his eyes wild now, turned, and fired once. Danny tripped and fell on his face and did not move.

Keele threw himself in the car and started the engine. He was pointing the wrong way and could get out only by making a wide circle. Ruža struggled for the gun in my hand. I released it because she was kneeling on my bad arm. She fired three times into his windscreen, and missed all three, and Marko was screaming: "Bastard, bastard!"

Then Keele was gone in a spatter of dirt. His offside front wheel ran over Danny's outstretched, reaching hand.

He was dead when we turned him over. Marko was sobbing, I thought mainly with anger, and Ruža was so quiet that I dared not look at her.

"Get him inside," she said softly.

"We'll have to get away from here," Marko cried.

"No. He won't be keen to report this, even though he could claim self-defence. He made a mistake, coming alone. Wanted all the credit. You!" That was me she meant. "Take his legs. Marko, you the shoulders. Inside, and quick about it."

The legs are the lighter end. I was pleased, but mainly that I didn't have to struggle, head down, over Danny's lifeless face. We got him inside and laid him on the long settle beneath the window.

"At least cover him up," I said, because Marko

seemed about to collapse.

Then Ruźa exploded in anger, whirling on me in a wild fury that whipped her hair into a whirl and her eyes into flame.

"This happened for you! He couldn't have taken you, not if you'd stood your ground."

"What you mean is—if I'd shot him."

"You fired over his head." She threw her hair back with a swipe of her knuckle.

Marko was looking sick. "I'll be out the back." But I wasn't paying any attention.

"What the hell did you expect?" I shouted at her. "You dragged me into this. I didn't want any of your Quayles and your robberies and your damned Comus conning me . . ."

"It wasn't him!"

"Somebody. Don't you glare at me like that, Ruźa. I'm not one of your heavies, chucking his weight about with a gun stuck in his fist. I'm just a bloke who got mixed up . . ."

"Liar!" she screamed.

"I'm only a photographer."

"Oh, of course you are!" Anger gave way to bitter sarcasm, which she produced close to a snarl. "You can take pictures. Very clever. But what sort of photographer have we got here?"

She leaned back against the table, hands supporting her each side, and eyed me up and down with measured contempt.

"Ruźa, what's this?"

"And he *still* pretends he doesn't know! After this last pretty little act!"

163

"Cut it out, will you." I couldn't stand that tone in her voice. She'd have cut less painfully with a whip.

"A fine actor, though. Fooled us all for a while."

"Would you please explain . . ."

"Do you want it straight—from the beginning? So clever with the theories, you are. You must think everybody else is stupid. D'you imagine we haven't been expecting something like this? Father said it was sure to happen some time."

I flapped my arms uselessly against my sides, quite forgetting the pain it would cause. Quite ignoring it when it came.

"What was it you expected?"

"With three years on the same caper—and seven weddings close to banks that'd been robbed—of course the police were going to connect up. So they'd try to plant a spy on us."

"Now just you wait . . ."

"*With* us, we thought, but when you order a photographer, and another turns up, then you get suspicious. And they've got photographers in the police. You can bet we gave it some thought. And what did you do! You popped up, all clean shining face, with the proofs in your hand, when they *always* send . . ."

"I'm new to this."

"New! You were raw. Easing your way into the house with your big-eyed act. We saw clean through you. Choke him off, said daddy. So Comus went out and got your negatives, and we thought we'd seen the end of you. But no . . . oh no. Then it really started. You obviously knew whose house you were in and what we did—"

"Will you just stop right there."

164

"I will not."

"I thought it was all a bit of fun, the double-bluff, you lot kidding me on . . ."

"Oh my God, fun he calls it. When my brother was dead and my husband was missing. And you came round playing games!"

"I'm sorry. I didn't want to hurt you."

"Oh no? Then why did you go on and on, persisting? You must have a skin like a buffalo, the way we tried to slide you off. But of course, I was forgetting—you were on duty."

"This is a complete distortion . . ."

"But who was it who could produce a police car when he needed it? Who could produce Martin's body!"

"But Ruźa . . ."

"And who pretended to get picked up, and handed his body in, and was out of that station again before you could eat an egg sandwich? Who was it sent that picture to Quayle, just to stir up trouble?"

Her face was red and hot, with the tears poised, her lower lip pouting like a hurt child on the verge of collapse. And yet with her head high and her voice like a lancet cutting into my soul.

"Not me, Ruźa," I breathed. "I swear . . ."

"All the fandango of the photographs. I suppose you enjoyed weaving patterns around those. You did. You did!" she flung at me. "The only thing we could do was keep Comus close to you so that you couldn't report to your blasted sergeant."

"Him! Ruźa, you're hysterical."

"And when you were hurt," she wailed, "and we took you in, you still had to go on with it and accuse dear

165

Comus of killing my brother."

She was distraught. I couldn't suffer her distress. But what words, now, could I use to persuade her, when it was clear, even to me, how it must have seemed to them? No wonder everybody had aimed their explanations at me!

I moved towards her. There was only one thing to be done, in whispers more sincere than protests. I spread my hands. "If you'll let me explain."

"Stop." I might have had the sense to remember her pistol. She produced it again. I paused.

"I gave you your chance," she said quietly. I could barely tell what she said, with her voice breaking. "You could have gone with your sergeant, in peace, but you had to go on playing games."

"Before I met you, the only thing I ever shot was a photograph, Ruźa. And I'm too short for the police."

She choked. "Keep your distance. I gave you a chance. Father said you weren't going to leave here alive."

I don't know how she managed to hold the thing so steadily, when her voice shook so much.

"Ruźa, I love you."

"Don't move."

I walked towards her and took her in my arms, and the gun was hard against my stomach. For a second she was stiff, then a sob shook her and I held her tight until it had gone, then the gun fell to the floor and I kissed her. Even during the day her lips were naked, and tasted of delight and freshness. I kissed her with my eyes shut, and tasted the salt of her tears, then opened my eyes to reach a finger and try to clear them and 'tice a smile, and beyond her shoulder I could see Marko, leaning in the back doorway, green and drained and barely able to clutch his gun.

"Ruźa!" I whispered.

"Dad said not alive," Marko pointed out. "Stand away from him."

# Thirteen

She tried to break free, but I held her firmly against me. For a second her eyes met mine in a blind, disbelieving look, then I turned her from between Marko and myself, and at last released her.

She was at once on her knees, reaching for the gun. I didn't dare allow that to continue. "No, Ruźa!"

Slowly she came to her feet. Despite what I'd said, she had the pistol in her hand. She laid it on the table close to me.

"Besides," I said, "you couldn't even hit a car. Between you, you'd wreck the place."

"Oh Christ!" Marko moaned. I didn't think he could even lift his gun.

"Ruźa," I said, not taking my eyes from Marko, "if I was a policeman, would I have spent half an hour trying to get your skin tone correct, your eyes, and that glint in your hair? They're over there in that wallet. Go and have a look."

"I noticed," she said softly.

"And would a policeman even trouble to keep his own set of proofs? Would he have his own wallets, a set of wallets, in his filing cabinet?"

"I believe you."

"And would a policeman, planted you say, *not* have got a picture of that man getting into the police car with your brother?"

There was silence. I turned. She had her hands to her face.

"I've got to sit down," said Marko.

"What's the matter?" I asked her, trying to part her fingers.

Words tangled in the choked breaths she struggled to take in.

"What is it?" I insisted.

"Quayle thinks you're a policeman. That's why he tried to persuade you that Comus was the man. My father thinks you're a policeman, and he's told you too much. And Sergeant Keele . . ."

"He *knows* I'm not."

"And now he'll want to arrest you—dead or alive. Lennie, what shall we do?"

I've never liked Lennie. It makes me sound immature, something I've always struggled to overcome. On her lips it was music.

"We've got to get to Comus," was all I could think.

"Comus," she said, "is *convinced* you're a copper."

"He's my friend."

"Oh Lord, but you're simple."

"He'll help us."

"You accused him. You threw everything back in his face."

"I was delirious."

"He was terribly hurt."

"There . . . doesn't that prove he's a friend?"

She looked at me with exasperation. Her manner was rapidly leaning towards the possessive. I wasn't sure I was keen on that, but at least it showed she had a certain amount of concern for my welfare.

169

"You don't," she said, "seem to have got it into your puddled head that everybody thinks you're an undercover policeman, from Special Branch or somewhere. Nobody feels safe with you around."

"But I'm harmless."

She laughed scornfully. Then sobered. "What do you want to do, then?"

"Certainly not wait here for things to happen. Find Comus."

Then Marko stirred. He had been fighting his way out of the shock of seeing his friend killed. He still had the gun, and as his father had expressed a lack of faith in his sons, he was now prepared to prove his worth. His grip on the gun was more purposeful.

"No," he said. "Father said he wasn't to leave here alive."

I didn't believe that Jovan could have put it like that. I was about to speak, but Ruźa put a hand on my arm. "Things have changed," she told him severely.

He was stubborn. "I don't see that. He was very clear."

"What exactly did he say?" I asked.

She turned on me. "You keep out of this." Then back to Marko. "I don't think he meant it like this."

"To me, he did. Sis, I wish you'd stop being awkward. Let's get it done with and go home."

"If he meant that," I put in, "he'd hardly have told me what he did."

"Such as?" Ruźa was distant and suspicious.

"That it was him who killed Martin, for one thing."

She sat down.

I tried again. "What were his exact words . . ." I

170

asked Marko.

"Did he *say* that?" she demanded. All the colour had left her lips.

"He told me that. Now, let's keep to the essentials."

"My father killed Martin?"

"What did he *say*, about me?"

She turned from me, her fist thrust against her lips. Marko put in: "He said you weren't going to leave here alive."

"Well then. It's the way you interpret it. A prediction, that's all it was. He reckoned half the county wants me dead, so he was pretty safe in saying . . ."

"Then it's up to me to make it come true."

But he wasn't keen, you could see. Not to do it coldly, without some sort of joyous conflict involved.

"He didn't *mean* that!" I cried.

He shook his head, the problem too heavy for him. I looked to Ruźa, but she was too involved with her own emotional struggle. I licked my lips.

"Then don't you think we should ask him for clarification?" I tried.

Ruźa stood purposefully. The pistol had disappeared from the table. "I've got to see my father."

I lifted my shoulders, only one palm raised because the other would not. "We'll all go and see him."

"Not you!" Marko shouted.

"Now look." Sweat was pouring from me. My left arm was aflame with agony. "You can take me to him with that gun in my kidneys, and ask him if he wants me dead—and then you can do it if he says yes. How's that?"

He shook his head desperately. "But then," he

pointed out, "you'll have left here, and it'll be too late."

It was too much. My nerves blew. I whirled Ruźa with my good arm, plunged my hand into the overlap of her skirt, and discovered where she had the pistol. I produced it and bounded at Marko, shouting something about his stupid stubbornness, and stuck the barrel under his chin. He was staring at me with his mouth open, appalled.

"Drop that gun!" I shouted into his face.

I was wild, gone too far. There could have been murder in my eyes; for a moment it was in my heart.

He dropped the gun. The snag at that point was that I couldn't pick up two guns, having only one good arm. I kicked the larger one away from him and tossed the small one to Ruźa.

"Now," I said, panting, "we'll leave here and ask your dad exactly what he meant about me. And we'll find Comus and ask him . . . ask him . . ."

It was as well she had got up from the chair. I stumbled across to it, very close to collapse.

Ruźa was full of commiseration. "Now look what you've done," she screamed at Marko. "His arm's bleeding again. Your arm's bleeding," she told me. "Sit still, I'll have to get something."

I sat very still after she had left the room, my eyes on Marko, my right fist resting on the table with his gun clasped in it. But he seemed resigned. More correctly, he was even relieved to have had the decision taken from him.

Ruźa returned with her arms full of repair materials. "There," she said. "Soon have you better." She was speaking in the absent, crooning voice of a mother to her

172

child. "Keep still, blast you!" Now she was speaking to me.

"Have you got anything to kill the pain?"

She had—morphine and a sealed syringe from dusty packs, indicating that her family of true heroes scorned pain-killers. She gave me a good shot, because I didn't.

"Now put it in a sling," I said.

The idea of that was to provide a hiding place and some support for Marko's pistol. When all was tied and all tucked away I felt better. More confident. You'd be surprised what a gun does to a man's personality.

We trooped out to my car, Marko carrying my hold-alls. I insisted on travelling in the back, Marko to drive with Ruźa beside him. In this way I felt I was in control, an illusion that passed only when I realised the strength of Ruźa's injection, and quietly passed out.

I cannot tell you the location of Beatings. Somebody had mentioned Gloucestershire, but it could have been anywhere in the Midlands. When I came round we were running through rolling countryside. The fine weather had deserted us, and grey sheets hid the hilltops. Marko had to put the wipers on a couple of miles further on. We plunged between steep banks to a village, through it, and began to climb.

"He's awake," said Ruźa. She turned. "Are you all right?"

I felt I had been on a long journey, and had barely retraced my steps in time. "Where are we?"

"A mile short of Beatings."

"You think your father'll be there?"

"There was some sort of a conference he was going . . ."

"I'm surprise those two don't get together. They're thick as thieves."

Marko laughed shortly, and took a left-hander that seemed to head into space.

We passed a side lane. I turned, looking back. "That was a police car."

"Yes." She sounded suddenly tense. "There's another, just behind that rise."

"They've got the place surrounded," I said.

"Two cars can't . . ."

"There's a whole gaggle under those trees."

"All right!" she said sharply.

"Don't you think we ought to turn back?"

"D'you imagine we could?"

"Shut up," said Marko. "I'm listening."

We had rounded a bluff. Beatings came into view. It stood on the top of a rise, one side of which was red with uncovered sand and gravel. He had taken a deserted range of buildings, previously the offices and operating sheds of a gravel pit, and converted it. The long, covered tunnel of the conveyor track was still visible, angling down into the old pit. The drive on which we were moving was gravel. There could be no hidden or silent approach to the buildings.

We came closer. I could see, now, the collection of cars spread along beneath the dirty windows of the offices. Sharply, a shot rang out. It was no more than a warning. Marko ignored it, as being the signal he'd been waiting for.

"They could pick us off if they wanted," he said in explanation.

We drew in. We got out of the car. All was silent. To

my right, the conveyor tunnel loomed high on a criss-crossed trestle of wood, a wooden staircase mounting its side.

"That's my father's car," said Ruźa.

"And the Landrover." I felt the nerves crawling between my shoulder blades. A voice spoke from the head of the staircase.

"You, stay where you are."

The rifle was centred on my chest. So he meant me. I was very still.

"The other two, inside. The door marked Private."

Ruźa and Marko disappeared from the periphery of my vision. I heard the door open and shut. I saw, my eyes focussing, that it was Cornelius Minnit behind that gun. There was an intensity of restraint in him that warned me to do nothing to disturb it. When I heard footsteps behind me I did not glance round. Hands reached under my arms and felt for a shoulder holster. They tried my belt, they investigated my pockets. They did not try the sling.

"Now move."

Oh dear, it was Carraway's voice. And it was clear that he was now using a certain amount of vision. I ventured: "I hope you've quite recovered."

"We gonna have a talk about that."

He prodded me, and I didn't have to guess with what. I moved. We went round the back, beneath the row of grimy windows, and he thrust me through a door with a self-closer. It closed on him. I plunged forward, but he gave a yell and came after me, and I was in a short corridor with a locked door at the end. He came up behind and clasped my injured arm. The morphine was wearing off. I was nearly down on my knees. He said:

175

"Funny!" Then he flung me through a side door, and the accuracy of his parting kick indicated that his eyesight was now completely recovered. I stopped in the middle of the room.

It had once served as an outside lavatory for the gravel workers. The toilet stalls and seats had been stripped out, forcibly, judging by the scarred walls. Three tiny windows, high up, supplied the only light. The dead end of a light cord drooped from the ceiling. Only one lavatory pan remained. Sitting on it was Sergeant Keele.

"What're *you* doing here?" I burst out.

"They picked me up, coming away from Ješić's farm."

"Danny's dead."

He grunted as though I'd kicked him, then managed a twisted smile. "Then it's a good job you were there."

"Is it?"

"Your evidence that it was self-defence. *Your* evidence, sir."

"What did you call me?"

"You'd be at least a Chief Inspector."

I leaned back against the wall. My arm was jumping about again, and I was so tired . . .

"Not you as well!"

"I wasn't sure if you'd come as an undercover man from Special Branch, brought in to trap the Ješićs . . ." His head was tilted, considering me. "But if it'd been that I'd have been told."

"I'm not a policeman," I said wearily.

"So it had to mean you'd come from Internal Investigations, checking up on me."

"I'm not interested in you."

"Oh, I admit I've been a bit unconventional—here

176

and there—you gotta bring 'em in. What else is there to the job? So I've brought 'em. Maybe they were a bit knocked about . . . maybe the odd one or two never made it to the station . . ."

"Self-defence?" I murmured.

"Yes, yes." His voice was eager. "I knew you'd understand."

"You've got it all wrong," I said desperately.

I was aching for him to get off that seat. I simply had to sit down. Keele's problems were a useless distraction to me.

"You don't understand, sir? But surely you realised why I've been keeping an eye open for you! Why'd I go alone to Comus Astel's bungalow? Keeping an eye open. You were taking a risk there, if I might say so, sir. But I was off duty. You can see, I wasn't going to let you get into trouble. I hope you'll remember that . . ."

"How many more times? I am *not* . . ."

"They ain't got it bugged, I'm sure, so this is off the record. You can be honest with me. After what I've done . . . that do at the Jeśićs' farm—you don't imagine I'd have gone on my own if I hadn't known you'd gone and put your neck in it. It was me'n you, then, sir. But I can take a tip. Why else did you fire over my head? It was a tip. You'd got it under control. I saw that. So I left."

"I've got next to nothing under control. I am not in your force!"

"You can tell me now, sir."

"I am *not* . . ." I sighed. "I'm not tall enough."

It got him off the seat. He considered me, blocking the way. "Oh, I don't know."

"I'm a lot shorter than you."

177

"I'm a couple of inches over the minimum."

"Well then."

"You're not standing up straight," he said severely. "Sir."

"I'm as straight as I can get," I croaked.

"Here . . . back to back. That's it."

Our questing fingers met above our respective heads.

"You're over two inches taller, Sergeant."

"It's my heels. Let's have our shoes off."

"I want to sit down."

"No, no. For me, sir."

"I don't think I can stay upright much longer."

He frowned in reproof. "It was you who said you're too short. *Now* try it."

We stood, back to back in our socks. His fingers reached. A pause.

"You're bending your knees," he said.

"I can't do anything else. You're bending yours. Stand straight."

"Half an inch," he said.

"A good two and a half."

"It depends on how you hold your head."

I turned. I drew back from him. My right hand was very close to the sling. I was going to have to shoot him to get to that seat.

He was eyeing me with concern. "You don't look well. Here, have my seat, sir."

He didn't realise he had just saved his life. I collapsed on it, my head in my right hand. After a few minutes:

"Cigarette?" he asked.

"No. What's going on?"

"We'll find out."

178

"You know there's half the county force out there?"

"Good for you, sir. You've got the lot trapped."

It was no good. You just couldn't talk to him. I sat and waited. Time drifted away. The door opened and Carraway appeared. He jerked a finger at me. "You." I got up and went past him. Minnit was waiting to escort Keele.

They now had the door open at the end of the corridor. I was thrust through it.

The room had once been a long office, a single-storey building constructed of breeze blocks between a steel framework, which laced nakedly above my head. Once, it had possibly vibrated with life when the desks were in and the phones going, the typewriters clattering. The desks were gone. They now had a row of foldable chairs along each side, Ješić's contingent seated down along my left, Quayle's to the right. Quayle had only seven men to Ješić's fourteen, but the balance was maintained by a heavier showing of firearms. Seated in the centre, between them, was Comus. An empty chair stood before me, facing down the room.

"Sit," said Carraway. I did. He went to take his seat beside Quayle. Minnit slouched past me, and sat by Carraway. Quayle fidgeted, and then asked me:

"Do you promise to tell the truth . . ." Nine weapons were aimed at me.

"The whole truth," put in Ješić, and three of his men showed me their guns.

"And nothing but," said Comus, whose hands were empty and who was very pale. And who was clearly on trial.

"We're after a bit of truth," said Quayle. "We're

179

gonna find out who went in that squad car and killed my two men and got the money."

"And who killed my son," said Ješić.

Comus laughed flatly. "And Len, mate, they've already made up their minds that it's me."

So I was the principal witness.

"Who else could it bloody-well be?" shouted Quayle.

Ješić stood, all gangling dignity. "Comus was at the reception. I want that on the record."

"Alibis!" Quayle howled. "You'd got that rigged, you cunning old bastard."

I could see that Ješić was in difficulties. As he'd killed Comus's brother, Martin, it was perhaps to his advantage to have Comus removed in case he forgot Ješić's claimed debt when he found out. And Quayle knew the truth. It was not, therefore, politic to provoke Quayle into that revelation, as Comus could still prove dangerous.

"The photographer was there," Ješić said. "Let him say."

Which threw it right in my face.

"The truth!" Quayle demanded. "Or Carraway blasts him out of that chair."

"I'm going to have order in this court," said a voice behind me. We'd have to have a judge, of course. But Quayle was slipping. He hadn't got a real one, only a minor representative of the law.

Keele sat in judgement. He grinned at me. His was the only chair with arms.

# Fourteen

I tried. There was no point in saying that I knew Comus had not been the man in that car, and had been framed. I couldn't prove it. I couldn't prove anything. I said:

"It's true I didn't see him at the reception. But I was busy. A photographer's a busy man at a reception. But there's the toast photograph."

Quayle crowed in triumph. "It proves nothing. Could've been some other guy, with his finger bent."

"Yes. But Comus made me blow it up from the negative. It was obvious when it proved nothing, even then. I was there, and I saw. He was wild."

"You're just sayin' that," Quayle cried.

"Of course I'm saying it," I said wearily. "I'm doing what I can for him. But there isn't much . . ."

I offered the apology to Comus. He inclined his head in thanks, but there was not much hope in his eyes. Somewhere along the line Quayle was going to decide he was their man, and as Ješić must know he wasn't, then the decision would be Ješić's, whether to intervene, or abandon Comus.

Comus spoke slowly. "If I'd been the man, then I'd have the money. Martin would've got his cut from me, without any killing."

"Now wait," I said, seeing it coming.

"But he came to you, Quayle," said Comus, "and you killed him."

"I did not. We arranged . . ."

"We?" Comus looked around. "Who arranged?"

Quayle's snide grin was a terrible thing. "Ješić came to me. He wanted to know who'd betrayed him. I told him. He said he'd deal with it."

Comus was still. "When was this?"

"He knew almost at once. He came before I knew my men were dead. He came—"

"So *that's* where he disappeared to!" Comus shouted.

"So you *were* at the reception!" I cried out.

There was a silence. Ješić came to his feet heavily. "You'll understand it had to be done, Comus. You'll know about discipline. I couldn't let a betrayal go unpunished."

"To encourage the others?" asked Comus softly.

"And so . . . if I have to betray *you*—then you'll understand . . ."

Comus laughed. "All my eighty-one alibis . . . are they going to swear I wasn't there? Is that it?"

"I can't afford to play it any other way."

"But he was there, at the reception," I put in angrily. "Surely you all heard what he said. Don't you understand what it means?"

"You're only making it worse, Len," said Comus.

"I'm trying . . ."

"One of them's got to kill me, anyway."

"I'm not having that. Now you lot, you can just listen to me. I can prove, from the photographs, that Comus was framed . . ." But my head was swinging, and if anybody had taken me up on it I couldn't have gone on.

Then I was aware that Ruźa had come to her feet. She had been so silent, sitting there next to Marko at the far end, that I had forgotten her. The only woman in the room, and I'd discounted her. This was an error. She advanced slowly into the centre of the floor and moved steadily towards Comus's chair. He was facing away from her. Her restrained dignity captured the silence.

"This man," she said, "is not fit to give evidence." And her accusing finger shot out, pointing directly at me. "He's not a fit person, because he's got the money himself."

"Ruźa!" I whispered.

But they all turned to stare at me.

"*He* was the man who got into that car with my brother Petar. *He* forced Petar into the chase—"

"But I was taking the photographs!" I shouted.

"No. Not you. Oh, it's clever. Nobody looks at the man taking the pictures, only at the people being photographed. Who have you ever known who could describe the photographer?"

Now, all twelve weapons pointed my way. I appealed wildly in all directions. "This is stupid!" But she was supporting herself against the back of Comus's chair, supporting herself because she was forcing herself to go on, and it drained her completely.

I appealed to her. "But *you* can remember the photographer, Ruźa. You spoke to me."

"No." Her voice caught.

"I can tell you the exact words."

"Which your stand-in told you. Lord, how you've fooled us! You've been the only one it couldn't be."

All eyes were on me. If there had not been the necessity to persuade me, next, to reveal where I had the money, all the trigger fingers would have been moving

183

too. Then I saw Ruźa's hand emerge from her skirt, and she dropped her pistol into Comus's lap.

"Now!" she shouted, and she rolled over backwards to get clear.

It was only a small pistol, but I've mentioned Comus's accuracy. He was there between them with a choice, and any hesitation would have cost him his life. A small hole appeared in the centre of Quayle's forehead. Always go for the leader. Oh yes, Comus understood all about discipline.

The room exploded. Carraway's sawn-off blasted heavily, and my chair disintegrated. I was no longer sitting in it, because I had slipped sideways, more in a half-faint than anything, and Keele had me up with a fistful of my shoulder.

"This way, sir."

I heard Ruźa scream. The room was resounding with a roar of almost continuous gun-fire. Comus was down on his face, crawling for cover.

"The car," I tried to shout.

"Sure."

Keele was heading back the way we'd come in. The car, too, was his thought, any old car so that it'd get us away from there. But I had a fixation. It had to be mine, because all my gear was in there, all my wedding negatives and the proofs . . .

Then suddenly, I knew I *could* prove that Comus was not their man. Just the thought of proofs had done it. "I can prove . . ."

"Come on," he snapped, forcing me into the corridor.

"I've got to get back . . . tell them . . ."

"It's too damn late to tell anybody anything."

I couldn't see that. My brain was swimming, and all I saw, with my famed photographic clarity, was the critical evidence I had. I fixed my eyes on that, my mind on it, and I was not aware that he had me out in the open air.

"Your car!" he shouted, and after all any old car wouldn't do.

He ran me, stumbling and dragging with my arm shrieking, round the building.

I raised my head. The fresh air attacked me. I saw that the horizon was sparking with police beetles as their cars edged over. From the building the shots were now sporadic. Two men staggered through the doorway marked Private and collapsed.

"Ruźa's in there," I said.

"We haven't got time—I can see the cars."

But I had left him, blindly, almost groping my way to the doorway. I had forgotten the pistol, still snug in my sling. I had no thought of fighting my way in. Jeśić appeared in front of me. Marko, his eyes staring, was clutching his arm with blood between his fingers.

"Ruźa's in there," I said.

"Comus has got her."

He turned and ran, Marko at his side. I pushed my way through the doorway on hands and knees, more because I couldn't stand than because I would present a smaller target. A bullet smacked into the doorway above my head.

They were against the wall, just inside. The air was thick with an acrid stink of gunsmoke and agony. Comus was crouched over her, and he'd found another weapon. There was no target visible.

"Her leg," he said. "Help me."

185

I couldn't even help myself. I offered my right arm. "Ruźa?" She smiled grimly. "It's my leg."

"I'll cover you," he said.

I slowly began to drag her along the floor. She moaned.

"I'd be better walking," she said.

"Keep your head down," Comus snapped, and he took a quick shot at a raised head to illustrate. I dragged on. It seemed an eternity.

"I can manage," she gasped.

"Only a few more feet."

"You're pulling my arm out."

We crawled, side by side, into the open air, where the sirens wailed upwards on the Doppler slope and the blue lights flicked against the approaching dusk.

I leaned, panting, against the wall outside. Ruźa clawed her way up my right arm until she was standing, favouring her left leg.

"It's only a scratch." But she was wincing.

I shaded my eyes. "There goes your father."

Ješić was half way down the steep slope where they'd worked the gravel from the hillside. He was slipping and sliding as the surface rolled beneath his feet, leaping in great gangling strides, with Marko matching him, hand still clasped to his other arm. They were heading down to where it levelled off, and where the shadows rushed to meet them on the valley floor.

"Where's Comus?" she said.

"He's coming."

"Your car . . . "

"Keele's getting it started."

"But *he'll* take us to the police."

I was confused. "No. Yes. Oh . . . hell."

The car engine fired. The nearest police vehicle was a quarter of a mile away. Comus came from the doorway, facing back and still firing.

"Run! Minnit's coming . . ."

We ran for my car. Keele was gunning the engine, looking back, all the doors open. He was grinning, some wolfish meaning in it. Ruźa fell in the back beside me. I sat on my hold-alls, wrenched them free, clutching the straps. Comus flung himself into the seat beside Keele.

"Let's go."

I looked back, and realised the urgency. Minnit had got his rifle. He leaned in the doorway, almost blinded by the blood streaming down his face, and steadied the gun. As Keele let in the clutch, Minnit fired. I heard the bullet strike the car.

"He's got the tank," I shouted, because I could smell petrol.

Keele fought the car, trying to get it round. He held full throttle in first, and we bounded forward. Another shot got a front tyre. The car lurched. Keele seemed to be losing control. We headed straight for the tangle of wooden legs supporting the conveyor tunnel. The car leaned as the slope took us. Keele twisted the wheel, but now we were lost, Ruźa screaming in my ear and Comus rigid against the light beyond the screen.

Then we struck and the car went up on edge, and stopped. Ruźa was on top of me, my arm an agony.

"Get the doors open," shouted Comus. "It's going up."

There was no way out my side. All I could do was lie there as Comus clambered free and forced the door open beyond Ruźa. He dragged her out and flung her free, then reached down for me.

"Not those damned hold-alls again!"

I dumbly offered them. He threw them behind him angrily, and reached down for me. All I had to offer was my weak right arm.

Flames were crawling along the side of the car when I got out. Keele was crouched, twenty feet away. Ruźa shouted for me. I crawled with Comus towards her. She held out a hand. She had my bags.

We turned. Beside me, Keele was in agony. I thought at first he'd hurt his wrist. Then suddenly he got to his feet with a roar of outrage and ran to the car.

"But I've got my bags," I shouted after him.

He did not hesitate. Already flames flickered along the grass at his feet. He flung himself at my buckled, wedged boot, and tore at it with his fingers. But he'd buckled it himself, hadn't he! It was his own fault. I could have laughed.

Then the tank blew up in his face and the flames consumed him. He turned, but he could only stagger in his torture. He was aflame. I steadied myself, and finally remembered my gun. I shot him twice in the chest, because I couldn't bear to see him suffer, and because he had killed Petar Ješić and Quayle's getaway men and taken the money. And because he was the only one who could have framed Comus.

# Fifteen

After I got out of hospital the first thing I did was check that I could still hold a camera to my eye. This I could do. The second was to console the cat, who had had to fend for himself so long. After a while and a half tin of food, he allowed me one quick stroke, then withdrew his favours in case he encouraged me too much.

I needed encouragement. I was sick with a sense of loss. Ruźa had vanished.

It was necessary to make up fresh developing solutions; they oxydise. I was tired. The first day out is always exhausting. But I was determined to get it done. All eighty-seven if necessary.

That was the full extent of the shots I'd taken at the wedding. Out of them there had been fifty-three reasonable ones. I had to see what was on the other thirty-four, to discover why the negatives had been so important to Sergeant Keele. After all, those I had printed as proofs had clearly not implicated him. But he'd tailed those negatives implacably.

There was nothing. Only one could have included him, and that the one taken by accident when I'd nearly knocked the tripod over. I could dimly detect that the blurred image included a car, and the bulk of a man running towards it.

It seemed a pity that it had all been for nothing. But the possibility had haunted him. I'd have liked to tell

189

Comus, but he was being held for questioning. I doubted they could charge him with anything. He hadn't done anything, not this time. But they'd surely need him as a Crown witness at the enquiry into Keele's activities, because Comus knew as well as I did the mistake Keele had made.

There had been only two sets of original proofs in existence, those in my wallet, which Comus himself had locked away in his safe, and those I had taken to Ruźa. So the print of the toast, sent to Quayle to frame Comus and to force him into producing the negatives in pure self-defence, must have come from the set I'd done for Ruźa, and which Keele had impounded.

That was no proof, of course, because other policemen had probably handled them. But Keele had had to have somewhere to hide the money, and my abandoned car would suggest one good hiding place, especially as he'd jammed the boot. That had been the final proof, that he'd risked his life—and lost it—in a final attempt to rescue the money, the previous one having failed.

This had been at Jeśić's place in Wales. There he'd tried for a hat-trick; me, the car, and the negatives. That failing, he'd gone for the bonus, Danny Summers. Ruźa hadn't been wrong about that, the police *had* planted someone in their midst, Danny. And Danny had dutifully reported the planned robbery to his Sergeant, and dutifully managed to show him the set of Ruźa's proofs, from which Keele had taken the crucial pair. It had therefore been imperative that Danny should be removed, before he thought about it too deeply.

Yes, Comus would give that evidence. But no amount of pressure would force him to reveal where Jeśić and

Marko had gone when they'd faded into that encroaching twilight. He'd know the Ješić haunts, their secret hideaways.

Some time, when he was free, I'd go to Comus and ask him where I might find Ruźa.

My buzzer went. I walked through into the studio, out on to the landing.

Ruźa was climbing my stairs. I backed. She was wearing the skirt I remembered, but with a blouse and a little jacket over it. She was coming up smiling.

"I didn't visit you in hospital," she said, not exactly apologising.

"No." I thought. "It's rather depressing."

"I thought I'd wait till you were out."

"Good idea."

"Why don't you stand still?"

I stood still. She came very close.

"Your father?" I whispered.

"He's well. Marko too."

"I'm pleased."

"Minnit was dead when they found him. You knew that?"

"I'd heard."

"So it doesn't matter that they think he shot Keele."

I attempted a smile. She laughed, put a finger to my lips and tried to smooth it. "You're nervous."

"You frighten me."

"Because of what I did at Beatings? But I thought you understood."

"Every eye was on me. Every gun."

"But you, you always work things out." She kissed the tip of my nose.

191

"I was nearly too slow." I studied her. She seemed unscarred by the experience.

"Will he be doing it again?" I asked. "Poppa Ješić and his wedding caper, I mean."

"He'll try it a few more times." She kissed my frown—both sides. "There's Ljubica. She's not married."

"Not even once?"

She threw her head back and really laughed. "Poor Lennie! Did you think I'd come looking for another husband? But I wouldn't ask you to do that."

"Wouldn't you?"

I seemed to take her in my arms. I think it was me.

"You're shaking," she whispered.

"I do when I'm scared."

She kissed me a few protracted times. "Still scared?" she asked softly.

"Scared you might not want a partner at all."

"That's better. I was afraid we were going to need a shotgun wedding."

"I was afraid you'd come armed."

She was soft against me. "I'm not armed," she breathed.

I checked. She wasn't. It was obvious why her pistol had been so warm.

Five minutes later the police came to question me about the theft of a developing tank from James Anthony Albright. I said I was busy, but I'd send it on to him. First class. Nothing less than first class for me.

As it was.